Marie von Ebner-Eschenbach

KRAMBAMBULI
THE DISTRICT DOCTOR

GERMAN CLASSICS

Marie von Ebner-Eschenbach

KRAMBAMBULI
THE DISTRICT DOCTOR

(Two Novellas)

With an Introduction by
John Preston Hoskins

MONDIAL

Mondial
New York

Marie von Ebner-Eschenbach:
Krambambuli. The District Doctor

German original titles:
Krambambuli. Der Kreisphysikus

With an Introduction about
"The Life of Marie von Ebner Eschenbach"
by John Preston Hoskins

Translation and Introduction based upon
the 1914 edition of "The German Classics.
Masterpieces of German Literature"
published by The German Publication Society, New York.
Editor (2008, Mondial): Andrew Moore

Translators:
Krambambuli: A. I. Du P. Coleman
The District Doctor: Julia Franklin

Cover image: *Marie von Ebner-Eschenbach* (1873),
painting by Karl Blaas.

ISBN 978-1-59569-104-0
Library of Congress Control Number: 2008935993

www.mondialbooks.com

THE LIFE OF
MARIE VON EBNER-ESCHENBACH

by
JOHN PRESTON HOSKINS

MARIE, FREIFRAU VON EBNER-ESCHENBACH, one of the foremost novelists in the German tongue, and one of the best short-story writers in the world, was born at Zdislavic in Moravia* on September 13, 1830. Her father, Count Franz von Dubsky, sprang from an ancient Bohemian family that had been settled in Moravia for about two centuries. Her mother, Countess Marie Vockel, a woman of very superior character, was of Saxon Protestant descent. German and Slavic blood is thus mingled in the novelist's veins in about equal proportions and to her lineage is probably due the fact that, in an epoch of race propaganda and race wars, she has risen above the din of contention and conflict to a cosmopolitan view of the world.

Little Marie Dubsky lost her mother in early infancy, but received a careful training from the third and particularly the fourth wife of her father. In accordance with the custom of the Austrian aristocracy she was taught at home by governesses, spending the winters at the town-house in Vienna and the summers at the Moravian family-seat. French, English, music, with a little drawing and modeling, were the chief subjects in which she received instruction. Her literary proclivities manifested themselves early. Anastasius Grün's romantic epic *The Last Knight*** was the first work that made a

---

* Region in today's Czech Republic; possession of the House of Habsburg until the end of World War I. - A.M.

** *Der letzte Ritter.*

I

deep impression upon her and she began in girlish fashion to improvise herself. Later the Burg Theatre in Vienna became her school. It was the last scions of the old classical drama, Friedrich Halm and Otto Prechtler, to whom she owed her inspiration. "On many such a consecrated evening," she tells us in her memoirs, "I sat on a little bench in the back of our box, my head burned, my cheek glowed, one cold shudder after another ran down my back, and I thought, 'sooner or later your productions will be performed here.' Those were hours! Each of them only strengthened my conviction that I was intended to be the Shakespeare of the nineteenth century." On the eve of her fourteenth birthday she writes with unsophisticated frankness to a former governess: "I am determined either not to live or to become the greatest poet of all peoples and times."

With youthful exuberance Marie Dubsky now devoted herself to poetry and produced an epic from Roman history, comedies, tragedies, short stories and miscellaneous poems, none of which have ever been printed. In 1847 some of her work was submitted by her stepmother to Franz Grillparzer. The Austrian dramatist was quick to recognize that she possessed genuine poetic talent and predicted: "To neglect the cultivation of this talent will hardly lie in the caprice of the possessor herself." Unfortunately he was not able to point out the right path for her development to follow. And the cloud of glory which played around the classics of the Burg Theatre proved a mirage alluring her for fifteen years into a course destined to end in bitter disappointment.

On her eighteenth birthday Marie Dubsky was married to a cousin, Moritz Freiherr von Ebner-Eschenbach, a man fifteen years her senior and a captain in the Engineering Corps of the Austrian army. Baron Moritz was a highly educated man whose scientific attainments had already won him a professorship at the Vienna Military

Academy. As an engineer, he made several inventions and furnished the plan for the demolition of the ancient city walls. In 1874 he was retired with the rank of Lieutenant Field-Marshal and traveled as far as Iceland and Persia. In his old age he wrote two stories based on reminiscences of Old Vienna, which artistically do not stand high but bear witness to an interesting personality.

Shortly after the popular uprisings of 1848 the Military Academy was removed to Klosterbruck, a former abbey, in the vicinity of Znaim. In this retired nook Frau von Ebner spent the next ten years of her life. Encouraged by her husband she devoted her mornings to comprehensive studies in history and literature and even took lessons from a German professor in logic and esthetics. Her enthusiasm for the drama was further stimulated by her intercourse with the playwright Joseph Weilen, at that time a teacher in the Military Academy. How many poems and plays she began and finished in this decade we may never know. They are all either lost or buried in the family archives. The only production that saw the light of publicity was a little volume: *From Franzensbad,* six epistles published anonymously in 1858 in which the follies of a fashionable watering-place are lashed with fiery indignation. The book is of no literary significance, but bears witness to the moral interpretation which the author has been ever wont to put on life.

In 1863 the Ebners returned to Vienna, which ever since has been the author's winter home. Here she soon lost sympathy with exclusive society and found her chief satisfaction in a small circle of chosen friends, particularly Ida von Fleischl and Betty Paoli, the lyric poet. As long as they lived, these two friends were the critics and counselors of all her literary plans and in their company she was accustomed weekly to enjoy her cup of tea and game of taroc. Her summers have usually been spent in industrious retirement at the beloved family-seat in Zdislavic with occasional sojourns in St. Gilgen and short trips to Germany to visit her most candid critic and correspondent, Louise von François, the novelist. After the death of her husband in 1898 she spent the two following winters in Italy.

In the year 1900 her birthday was celebrated all over Austria and Germany. Thousands of congratulations were received from her admirers everywhere. An address with ten thousand signatures was presented to her and a medal struck in her honor. As a crowning distinction, in this same year the University of Vienna conferred upon her the degree of Ph.D. *honoris causa...* : "To Marie von Ebner-Eschenbach, the incomparable story-teller, the greatest woman writer in the German tongue, the first among the living writers of Austria, the wise and charitable judge of life," — thus begins her patent of academic nobility.

Marie Ebner's work is divided by the year 1875. Previous to that date she devoted herself to the drama, after it almost exclusively to fiction. The year 1885 is also of significance in her fiction. As an artistic nature that matured slowly she was over fifty before she attained her full powers and produced her profound studies of life in forms of almost flawless excellence.

A satisfactory account of Frau von Ebner's dramas has still to be written. None of them have ever been included in her published works, pretty good evidence that her own mature judgment regards none of them of lasting value. Why she failed as a playwright is not easy to answer. The accounts of her plays that were actually performed are very conflicting. That she possessed a certain rhetorical virtuosity, even Otto Ludwig, the champion of the realistic drama, acknowledged. That she possessed also a certain power of characterization, as well as a decided vein of comedy, a gift rare in women, seems equally certain. But her enthusiastic admiration for the old classical tragedy seems to have blinded her to the fact that this type was no longer a productive species. A new realistic movement was setting in upon the stage. For this she seems to have had no understanding. The fact, too, that she did not acquire skill in developing a plot until late in life, even in her fiction, warrants the inference that there must have been serious structural defects in her dramas. In comedy, with all her facility in dialogue, she had nothing new to offer in her characters and situations, while her satiric and didactic tendencies were too pronounced to meet the favor of the public.

Her best known dramas are: *Mary Stuart in Scotland,* a tragedy accepted by Eduard Devrient in 1860 for the Karlsruhe theatre; *Marie Roland,* a tragedy of the French Revolution, written in 1867, but never performed; *The Violets* (1863), a satire on polite lies, which later enjoyed a short run in Berlin; *Dr. Ritter,* a one-act dramatization of Schiller's well known sojourn in Bauerbach, written for the Schiller festival in 1869, and *A Forest Nymph,* a very sharp satire on aristocratic society, which was received by the Vienna press with a blast of censure when performed in 1873.

Marie Ebner ... did not attain the success in the drama of which she had so fondly dreamt. But she was not a spirit to be utterly dismayed. She wrestled with her sorrow until it blessed her. Slowly she came to a knowledge of her own limitations and recognized that her true mission lay in a different field. For over twenty years the short-story had been successfully cultivated in Germany by such writers as Gotthelf, Auerbach, Storm, Reuter, Keller, and Paul Heyse. Turgueniev, in French translations, was gaining a European reputation. Influenced chiefly by Heyse and Turgueniev, Frau von Ebner now abandoned the tragic stage of history to confine herself to the depiction of that with which she had been familiar from her childhood, the life of the Austrian aristocracy in town and country.

Even in the field of fiction Marie Ebner had to struggle for almost a decade before she won a place in the public esteem. Her first fairy-tale, *The Princess of Banalia* (1872), a vague satire, her first book of *Tales* (1875), and her first novel *Božena* (1876), were scarcely noticed by the public press. After the appearance of *Božena,* Baron Cotta is said to have vowed never again to publish anything written by a woman. The five stories included in her volume of *Tales* are now chiefly of biographical interest, but *Božena* is a very noteworthy performance. This Moravian maid-servant that serves three generations in the same family, that has the courage openly to confess her sin and to break with a snap from her seducer, that travels on foot with her foster child from Hungary to Moravia and by sheer force of character compels the designing step-mother to grant the child her rightful inheritance, is a figure worthy of Gotthelf or of Keller. In spite, however, of the vivid characterization and the accurate pictures of Moravian life, the style is prolix, the motives tangled and the work as a whole very faulty in structure.

The next story published by Marie Ebner marks the turning point in her popularity. *Lotti, the Watchmaker* (1880), was accepted by the *Deutsche Rundschau,* the leading literary monthly, and with a bound the author at fifty took her place among the foremost story-writers. In *Lotti,* one of the author's few stories dealing exclusively with bourgeois life, the unpretentious watchmakers who carry on their craft as an art are glorified in contrast to the life of notoriety and sensation led by a fashionable writer who follows his art as a business. In spite of a surer sense of detail and an artistic conscience which shrinks at no effort, this story shows some of the looseness and prolixity of her earlier tales. The action moves slowly and in the character of the heroine there is an excess of goodness, as there is in Claire, the heroine of *Again the Same Old Self* (1885), a better story on a somewhat similar theme.

Marie Ebner's reputation was now established and in the hostility to everything sensational, everything false, everything base, manifested in *Lotti,* lay, as it were, the whole future program of the novelist. During the next two decades tales and novels follow in rapid succession.

The author grouped her stories in seven volumes under the titles: *Tales* and *Stories of Village and Manor-House.* The second title aptly describes almost everything she wrote after 1880. The Austrian aristocracy with their Slavo-German dependents in the Moravian villages constitute the world of her fiction. Country and city are her theatres, noble and peasant keep the balance. Her time is usually the immediate present, seldom — as in *He Kisses Your Hand* (1885) — does she turn to the brutal customs and smug gallows' humor of the past. All forms of the short-story are at her command; letters, diaries, dialogues, and that most difficult of all forms, the story within a story. In them all there is goodness without effeminacy, sympathy without sentimentality, benignity without cant, and that ever sparkling humor which banishes every trace of monotony.

Who can ever forget *The Barons of Gemperlein* (1881), her first great triumph in humor, these quixotic barons, the one feudal, the other radical, both shipwrecked matrimonial candidates, both obstinate and hot-headed, but both nobly good? Or that most soul-breathing of all her stories, *After Death* (1882), told with a refinement and delicacy of feeling that recalls the tone and technique of Storm? Where can be found a more concrete and genial characterization of the leading political lords and ladies, more lifelike portraits of officialdom and of the much abused peasantry than in her two historic tales: *The District Doctor* and *Jacob Szela* (1883), which have as their background the bloody peasant uprisings in Galicia* in

---

* Galicia is a historical region in East Central Europe, divided between Poland and Ukraine. - A.M.

1846? Where do we find human sympathy ethically and artistically more refined than in her little masterpiece *Krambambuli* (1883), the story of a dog with spotless pedigree who, like Rüdiger in the *Nibelungen,* perishes in the vain attempt to serve two masters? What humane social tolerance pervades her account of the sporting *Comtesse Muschi,* superficial, but jauntily frank and sincere, who tells her story in breezy letters; and of the more studious *Comtesse Paula* (1884), who dares to be inelegant and devotes herself seriously to the production of memoirs. Everything in these self-confessions is so natural, so full of life and truth and freshness that we easily overlook the art by which they are produced.

In the year 1886 Frau von Ebner published her second novel: *The Child of the Parish,* a tale of Moravian village life. This book depicts the struggles of a waif who, under the most adverse conditions both of temperament and environment, gradually fights his way to a position of thrift and respectability. The story begins with the sober narrative of a murder trial and ends, as it were, with the transfiguration of a saint. This novel is more than an interesting study in child psychology. It is more than a protest against the hereditary curse of sin. It does more than brilliantly formulate a social problem. It is a call to a firmer belief in the goodness of human nature, in the power of education, and especially in the possibilities of self-reliance and self-help. The pupil of Gotthelf and Auerbach here unites the characteristics of the realistic and idealistic village-novel in a higher synthesis. We shudder when we think what a pupil of Zola would have made of such materials.

This novel also marks the vast strides which the author had made during the last ten years in all that concerned her art. She had become more realistic, avoided more and more everything improbable and affected, everything sentimental and prudish. She saw life more steadily, she observed more sharply and chose the essential and the significant with greater accuracy. The structural defects of her earlier works were eliminated. Here we find that clarity, harmony and unity of presentation, that concentration and condensation of the action that marks the great artist. She is still of the conviction that it is not the business of art to give a photographic reproduction of life, but that the divine fire of the artist must purify the materials and transmute them into a work of beauty.

In striking contrast to the happy atonement in *The Child of the Parish* stands *Beyond Atonement* (1889), a gloomy picture of remorse in the soul of a high-born aristocrat. The heroine, the young Countess Maria Wolfsberg, has married the model cavalier Count Dornach after her father had rejected another suitor for whom she had a deep affection. She becomes a model wife and mother, but in an unguarded moment this former suitor succeeds in entrapping her and she yields to his passion. Now the guilt rests upon her. The book is the history of her remorse. She tries to stifle her feelings by acts of benevolence, by social distraction; naught avails. She seeks the consolations of religion without finding peace. In a sudden accident she loses both her husband and her eldest son. Only the youngest is left, the testimony of her guilt. She openly confesses her transgression. A mortal illness ends her suffering. "All is lost—faith in Providence — faith in my own free will — and yet only one wish—O! that I had never done wrong!" are her dying words.

The question how the guilt of a woman could be atoned had already occupied Marie Ebner in her dramatic period. With riper experience and more consummate art she takes up the question again. Her answer in this case has been the subject of much discussion. Few American readers will be entirely reconciled to Maria's fall, fewer are likely to agree with her own final conclusion that her sin is beyond atonement. Nevertheless, on none of her works has the author expended more love and effort. Artistically it is her finest production and deserves to rank with the great novels of the century. Louise von François called it a German *Anna Karenina*. Structurally this novel is superior to Tolstoy's masterpiece; as a searching study of human life hardly so convincing.

In 1892 the author dedicated to her dear friend Ida Fleischl a little volume of *Aphorisms, Parables, Fairytales and Poems*. Of her poetry it may be said that it is chiefly of biographical interest, it lacks fire and it has no wings. Her parables and fairy-tales are only the elaboration of her aphorisms with severer ethics and more biting criticism. In her aphorisms Marie Ebner has concentrated the very quintessence of her philosophy of life and art. They are not brilliant paradoxes, the witty play of the understanding in a spirit of egotistical aloofness and abstraction. But they represent the fruits of a rich experience, of deep self-study, of intellectual battles joyfully undertaken, and of a searching of conscience victoriously carried through. They are written with a pen dipped in her own heart's blood.

During the last ten years of her literary activity the works of Frau von Ebner grow more profound. For the problem-novel which charged the literary atmosphere with "burning" questions during this decade, she has little sympathy. With that largeness, freedom, insight, and benignity which characterizes the older idealism of Goethe and Schiller, she is deeply concerned only with those more fundamental and universal problems of the human soul which lie at the very foundation of all education, art, and religion ...

The deepest and most significant of the tales that were written in what has been called her *terzia maniera* is the novelette *Without Faith?* (1893), another story of village life, this time in the Austrian Alps. A young country priest on the verge of losing his faith in God, not as the result of scientific investigation, nor of the higher criticism, but in consequence of the terrible human depravity which he finds in his parish, finally substitutes for his ecclesiastical creed a faith in humanity and decides to remain in his parish, content with a modest activity in a narrow circle.

Artistically this novelet is one of the author's best, but as is usual in the case of most novels dealing with religious problems, the question is not settled. The hero's conflict ends in an interrogation point, and his future course is determined solely by temperamental considerations. Perhaps a more heroic outcome was not to be expected on Austrian soil. But in any case, the tale is significant of the vast change that has come over religious thinking even in Roman Catholic countries.

That the author, however, could think through such questions to a conclusion is proved by the modern tragedy in *The Baleful** (1894). A father placed before the difficult choice of saving his only daughter's life by a single word, or of sacrificing her to the bullet of an avenging murderer, lets fate take its course in order that "the Baleful" may be rooted out of the world. With similar indignation the author in *Missing* (1895), and in *Bertram Vogelweid* (1896), turns on the harmful in art. "An artist—a priest" is the author's creed. In the first, an old painter outraged by the hue and cry of the naturalists, retires from the world only to be sought out by one of his former colleagues, a boastful pretender of the modern school. In the second, with far greater whim and humor the author makes short shrift of Nietzscheanism, the young Czech movement, the erotic mania and all other types of *fin de siècle* poetry, often in terms more expressive than elegant. Other stories of this decade are *The*

---

* A term applied by hunters to destructive animals.

Favored Pupil (1892), which pictures the woes of a poor gymnasium student; *Oversberg* (1893), a flawless example of the author's skill in telling a story within a story; the tragic *Death Watch* (1893), in which the whole fate of a man — past, present, and future — is condensed into a single scene; and that charming idyll *Miss Susanna's Christmas Eve* (1902), in which the author embodies a picture of her own generosity.

Marie von Ebner-Eschenbach ... has been called a realist, but she is a realist only in her wonderfully sharp power of observation and in the fact that she does not avoid the commonplace and the ugly. She is at heart an idealist who is always seeking the eternal and universal significance of these every-day commonplaces. Her literary significance lies in the fact that in an age whose art is permeated with a spirit hostile to religious faith and morality, she, without pedantry, without sentimentality, without cant, has lifted up the banner of idealism in life and art and once more united the German literature of the last quarter of the nineteenth century with the literature of the classic period.

Of the qualities that make up a great writer she has the deep and high truth of substance. She does not view the world in the rosy light of the idyll. She never seeks to avoid the ugly. She goes after guilt great and small. But more, she puts a high moral interpretation on human life. Her ethics is proof against all egotism and will bear comparison with that of the great moralists, ancient and modern. To her the soul is everything, externals nothing. She does not describe persons, but through small characteristic actions almost imperceptibly conjures up the personality like a vision. In this method she is without a peer since Goethe. It is her style which is not free from shortcomings. Her diction is plain and almost colorless. Her expression often suffers from a certain harshness and uncertainty disturbing the narrative. To settings she pays little attention and her work is lacking in lyric appeal.

Marie Ebner has often been compared to George Sand and George Eliot. She has neither their imaginative power nor their proselytic zeal. But she is a truer interpreter of life than the former, and has a finer feeling for structure than the latter. Her closest kinship is with Turgueniev, without his sympathy for weak-willed men of feeling and without his fatalism. She is not so prolific as any of these three, but it is not improbable that a larger fraction of her works will live.

KRAMBAMBULI

A MAN may have a kind of liking for all sorts of things and all manner of creatures; but love—the real thing that does not pass away—he learns to know, if at all, only once in his life. This, at least, is the conviction of Ranger Hopp. How many dogs has he had in his time, and liked them too! But to love—what you can really call to love—and never to forget, only one: Krambambuli. He bought him, or more strictly speaking traded him, in the "Lion" tavern at Wischau, from an under-forester out of a job. The very first time he looked at the dog, he was taken with a liking for him that was to last as long as he lived. The master of the handsome beast, sitting at the table by an empty brandy-glass and grumbling at the landlord because he would not give him another, looked like a thorough rascal. He was a little fellow, still young and yet as dried up and weather-beaten as a dead tree, with yellow hair and a scanty yellow beard. His forester's coat, probably a relic of the departed splendors of his previous service, bore traces of a night spent in wet ditches by the roadside. Although Hopp was not fond of bad company, he took a seat near the fellow and began at once to talk with him. He soon found out that the good-for-nothing drunkard had already pledged his gun and his game-bag to the landlord, and was now inclined to let the dog go the same way; but the landlord, wretched usurer, refused to hear of a pledge that would need to be fed every day.

At first Herr Hopp said no word of the liking he had taken to the dog, but called for a bottle of the good Danzig cherry brandy which the landlord had, and made haste to pour some out for the vagabond. In an hour all was settled. The ranger handed over twelve bottles of the liquor on which the bargain had been struck—the other

1

gave up the dog. To his credit be it said, it was not easy for him. His hands trembled so as he fastened the cord about the animal's neck that it seemed as if he would never finish the operation. Hopp waited patiently, admiring the wonderful quality of the dog, in spite of his bad condition. He was not more than two years old; his coloring corresponded to that of the wretch who was abandoning him, though perhaps a couple of shades darker. On his forehead he had a mark, a white streak that ran off in slender lines to right and left, like pine-needles. His eyes were big and black and lustrous, ringed about with clear amber; his ears sat high, long and perfect. In fact, there was not a flaw in the whole dog, from the tips of his paws to the end of his fine, sensitive nose. The whole supple and yet powerful frame was beyond praise, borne on four living columns that might have supported the body of a deer and were not much thicker than a hare's legs. By St. Hubert the creature must have had a pedigree as long and as pure as that of a knight of the Teutonic Order.

The ranger's heart exulted over the splendid bargain he had made. He stood up, took the cord which the vagabond had at last succeeded in tying, and asked "What's his name?"

"His name—? Why, you can call him the same as what you've bought him for—Krambambuli!"

"Well, Krambambuli it shall be. Come on, then! Are you ready? Off we go!"

But no matter how he called and whistled and pulled, the dog refused to obey. He turned his head toward the man whom he still regarded as his master, only whined when the latter shouted "March!" and accompanied the order with a vigorous kick, and still tried to huddle close to him. Only after a hard struggle did Herr Hopp succeed in taking possession of the dog. Finally he had to be tied up, put in a bag, and carried off on his new master's shoulder to the hunting-lodge which lay several miles away.

It took two full months before Krambambuli, beaten half to death, and chained with a spiked collar after each attempt at flight, at last came to understand to whom he belonged. But then, when his subjection was completed, what a dog he was! No tongue can describe, no word can measure the height of perfection that he reached—not merely in the exercise of his appointed functions but in his daily life as a zealous servant, a good comrade, a true friend and guardian. It is often said of intelligent dogs that nothing is lacking to them but the power of speech; to Krambambuli not even this was lacking—his master, at least, was able to hold long conversations with him. The ranger's wife became actually jealous of "Buli," as she called him scornfully. Sometimes she reproached her husband. She had spent the whole day in silence at her monotonous knitting, when she was not sweeping, washing, or cooking. At night, after supper, when she picked up her knitting again, she would have been glad of a bit of a chat.

"You've always got something to say to Buli, Hopp, and never anything to me! Talking to a dumb brute the way you do, you'll forget how to talk to humans!"

The ranger admitted that there was something in what she said, but he saw no remedy. What was he to talk to his old woman about? They had never had any children; they were not allowed to keep a cow; and a gamekeeper finds no interest in domestic fowls when they are alive, and not much when they are cooked. The breeding or shooting of game, on the other hand, she knew nothing about. Finally Hopp found a way out of the difficulty. Instead of talking *to* Krambambuli, he talked *of* Krambambuli—of the triumphs that he won everywhere, of the envy that the possession of him excited, of the absurdly high sums that had been offered for him and contemptuously rejected.

Two years passed by in this manner. Then, one day,

the Countess, his master's wife, appeared at the ranger's door. He knew at once what the visit must mean; and when the kind and beautiful lady began "Tomorrow, my good Hopp, is the Count's birthday—" he took up the sentence quietly with a smile: "And your gracious ladyship wishes to make him a present—and you have come to the conclusion that you couldn't give him anything else as good as—Krambambuli!"

"Yes, yes, my dear Hopp—you've guessed it!" The Countess flushed with pleasure at finding him meet her half-way, spoke of her gratitude, and begged him to name the price that should be paid for the dog. The wily old ranger chuckled, put on an exceedingly deferential air, and presently came out with a decisive declaration.

"Please your ladyship, if the dog stays at the Castle, if he doesn't bite through every cord and break every chain, or strangle himself trying, then your ladyship may have him for nothing—for that is just what he would be worth to *me.*"

The test was made; but it did not go as far as strangling, for the Count, before that point was reached, lost all pleasure in the obstinate creature. It was useless to try to win him by kindness or to conquer him by force. He snapped at every one who came near him, refused to eat, and (for a hunting-dog has not much reserve flesh) wasted away to a skeleton. In a few weeks Hopp got word to come and take away his worthless cur. When he speedily responded to the summons and sought the dog in his kennel, there was a meeting full of indescribable joy. Krambambuli uttered a feeble bark, jumped on his master, put his fore-paws against his breast, and licked away the tears of joy that were running down the old man's cheeks.

On the evening of this blissful day, the pair paid a visit to the tavern. The ranger played cards with the doctor and the steward; Krambambuli lay in the corner by his master's chair. Now and then Hopp looked round at him, and the dog, no matter how sound asleep he seemed to be, instantly began to thump with his tail on the floor, as if he would say "Here I am!" And when Hopp, carried away by joy, shouted out as if it were a song of triumph, "How goes it with my Krambambuli?" the dog rose with respectful dignity, stood at attention, and answered with his clear eyes, "It goes well!"

About this time, not only in the Count's preserves, but in the whole surrounding district, a band of poachers carried on their operations in the boldest fashion. The leader was a dissolute rascal. He was called "Yellow" by the wood-cutters who met him drinking his brandy in some tavern of ill-repute, the game-keepers who now and then got on his track, though they could never come up with him, and the customers whom he had for his ill-gotten booty among the lowest class in every village.

He was the most daring rogue that ever set a problem for honest game-keepers. He must have been at one time in the profession himself, or he would never have known how to track out the game with such accuracy or so cleverly to avoid every trap that was set for him.

His depredations reached an unheard-of height, and all the men employed on the estate were grimly bent on catching him. Thus it happened only too often that those who were caught in some small breach of the game-laws were more roughly treated than at another time they would have been or than could quite be justified. This caused a great deal of bitterness in various places. The head gamekeeper, against whom the feeling was strongest, received not a few well-meant warnings. The poachers, it was said, had taken their oath to make an example of him the first good chance they got. The bold, high-spirited man, however, tossed these warnings to the winds, and took all the more care to let it be known that he had enjoined the greatest strictness on his subordinates, and was prepared to take the entire responsibility for any unpleasant consequences. Most frequently he reminded Ranger Hopp of the need for strict execution of his duties, and sometimes reproached him for lack of sharpness — at which, however, the old man only smiled. But Krambambuli, at whom on such occasions he looked down with a wink, yawned loudly and contemptuously. He and his master bore no grudge against the head game-keeper, who was the son of the memorable hero that had taught Hopp all the noble lore of the chase, as Hopp in turn had initiated the game-keeper when a boy into the same calling. The ranger still thought with pleasure of the trouble he had taken with his education, was proud of his former pupil, and loved him in spite of the rough handling which he, as well as the others, got from him.

One June morning he met him again in the act of administering justice.

It was in the circular clearing among the lime-trees, at the end of the park on the border of "the Count's Wood," and in the neighborhood of the breeding-places, which the head game-keeper would have liked to protect with murderous mines. The trees were at their best just then, and a dozen small boys had climbed into their branches. Nimble as squirrels they swarmed over the limbs of the splendid trees, broke off all the smaller branches within their reach, and threw them on the ground. Two women quickly picked them up and stuffed them into baskets, which were already more than half full of the fragrant spoils. The head game-keeper flew into a terrible rage, and ordered his subordinates to shake the boys out of the trees, regardless of the height from which they fell. While they crawled to his feet with cries and lamentations, one with the skin scratched off his face, another with a dislocated shoulder, a third with a broken leg, he gave the two women a sound drubbing with his own hands. In one of them Hopp recognized the light hussy whom rumor pointed out as the mistress of "Yellow." And when the women's baskets and shawls and the boys' hats had been seized and Hopp was charged to produce them before the court, he could not get rid of an unpleasant foreboding.

The order which the head keeper, wild as a devil in hell and surrounded by wailing and tortured sinners, shouted to him then, was the last he ever had from him. One week later he came face to face with him again in the circular clearing among the beech-trees — dead. From the appearance of the body it was plain that it had been dragged here, through mud and underbrush, that it might lie in state on this very spot. It had been placed upon a pile of broken boughs, the forehead encircled with a chaplet of blossoms, and another wreath of the same sort laid across his breast. His hat was by his side, also filled with blossoms. The murderers had left him his game-bag too — only they had removed the cartridges and replaced them with more blossoms. His fine breech-loader was missing; in its stead was a worthless old musket. When, later, they found the bullet that caused his death, buried in his breast, it fitted exactly the barrel of this weapon which had been laid in mockery across his shoulder. Hopp stood petrified with horror, gazing down at the disfigured corpse. He was unable to lift a finger, and even his brain seemed paralyzed; he could do nothing but stare and stare, and it was only some moments later that he regained his power of observation and asked himself a silent question — "What's the matter with the dog?"

Krambambuli was sniffing at the corpse, and running about distractedly, his nose on the ground. Once he whimpered, once he uttered a shrill yelp of joy; then he gave tongue and made a few quick leaps, just as if a long slumbering memory had awaked in him.

"Down!" cried Hopp, "Down with you!" And Krambambuli obeyed; but he gazed at his master with intense
excitement, and (as Hopp would have expressed it) *said*
to him, "For goodness' sake, don't you see anything!
Don't you smell anything? Oh, master dear, do look — do
smell! Master, come — come this way!" And he thumped
with his tail against the ranger's knee, stole back to the
corpse, often looking round as if to say, "Do you follow
me?" and began to take the heavy gun in his mouth,
plainly trying to lift it.

A shudder ran down the ranger's spine, and all kinds
of conjectures began to dawn in his mind. But because
it was his business, not to see millstones, not to give instruction to the authorities, but rather to leave untouched
the ghastly thing he had found and go his way, which in
this case led straight to the ministers of justice — well, he
did just what it was his business to do.

After all the formalities prescribed by the law in the
case of such a catastrophe had been fulfilled, which took
the whole day and part of the night, Hopp found time
before he slept for another conversation with his dog.

"Old dog," he said, "now the police are at work, and
they'll be skirmishing about all over the place. Are we
going to leave it to others to rid the world of the black-
guard that killed the chief? My old dog knows the low-
lived villain — yes, yes, he knows him! But nobody needs
to know that — I haven't told 'em. Ha! ha! I think I'll
bring my dog into the job — there may be some sport!"
He stooped over the dog, who sat between his outspread
legs, and pressed his cheek against the animal's head,
taking his grateful caresses in return. Then he went on
murmuring, "How goes it with my Krambambuli?" until sleep overtook him.

Psychologists have attempted to explain the mysterious impulse that drives many criminals to return again
and again to the scene of his crime. Hopp knew noth-

ing of their learned disquisitions; but none the less he scouted incessantly, with his dog, in the neighborhood of the circular clearing.

On the tenth day after the head keeper's murder he had for the first time given a few hours' thought to something else than his vengeance, and had been busy in "the Count's Wood" marking the trees which were to be taken down at the next cutting.

When he had finished his task, however, he threw his gun over his shoulder once more and took the shortest way through the woods to the breeding-places near the circle. At the particular moment when he set foot on the path that runs along the side of the beech-wood, he fancied he heard something rustle in the underbrush. A moment later silence reigned again—a deep, continuing silence. He would almost have thought there had been nothing to take note of, if the dog had not looked with such special keenness into the thicket. His hair bristling, his neck outstretched, his tail stiff, he glared at one particular spot in the undergrowth. "Oho!" thought Hopp, "if that's you, my fine fellow—just wait!" He slipped behind a tree and cocked his gun. His heart beat wildly in his bosom, and his naturally short breath came near failing him entirely—when suddenly, wonderful to relate, "Yellow" came through the hedge on to the footpath. Two young hares were hanging from his bag, and on his shoulder the headkeeper's breechloader with its Russialeather straps. It was a strong temptation to shoot down the villain from the safe concealment.

But Hopp was not the man to fire upon even the worst offender without first warning him. With one bound he sprang out from behind the tree and on to the path, crying, "Give yourself up, you cursed rascal!" As the poacher, for his only answer, snatched the gun from his shoulder, the ranger pulled the trigger. Good heavens! a flash in the pan! a harmless crack instead of a heavy detonation! The loaded gun had been left too long leaning against a tree in the damp woods.

"Good-by—so this is death!" thought the old man. But no—he is still unwounded; only his hat flies off, riddled with shot. The other, too, has no luck today—that is the last cartridge in his gun, and he must pull another out of his pocket.

"At him!" cries Hopp hoarsely to his dog—"Seize him!"

"Here, Krambambuli—here to me!" calls the other with a soft and coaxing voice—ah, a well-known voice!

And the dog. * * * * What happened next took less time to happen than to relate.

Krambambuli had recognized his first master, and ran toward him—half the way. Then Hopp whistled, and he turned; "Yellow" whistled, he turned again—quivering in desperate uncertainty on a spot equally distant from the two men, attracted at once and repelled.

Finally the poor beast gave up the hopeless conflict, and put an end to his doubts, but not to his suffering. Baying, howling, his belly on the ground, his body taut as a sinew, his head raised as though he were calling on heaven to witness his torture, he crawled—to his first master.

At the sight a thirst for blood seized Hopp. With trembling fingers he had put in a fresh cartridge; with calm sureness he took aim. But the poacher had once more raised his barrel to point it at him. This time it would be decisive! Both of them knew this—and, whatever thoughts were going through their minds, they faced each other as calmly as if they had been painted on canvas.

Two shots rang out. The keeper hit, the poacher missed.

And why? Because, as the dog leaped upon him with excited caresses, he started at the moment of pulling the trigger. "Beast!" he hissed between his teeth, then fell backward, motionless.

The executioner came slowly toward him. "You've had enough," he was thinking; "'twere a pity to waste another bullet on you." Nevertheless, he set his gun on the ground and loaded it anew. The dog sat up straight in front of him, his tongue hanging out, panting quickly and loudly, and gazing at the ranger. And when he had finished his loading and picked up his gun once more, they held a colloquy of which no witness could have understood a word, had a living man been there instead of the dead.

"You know for whom *this* bullet is meant?"

"I can guess."

"Deserter—traitor—vile scum, forgetful of all faith and duty!"

"Yes, master—that I am."

"You were my joy once. But now it is all over. You are no more to me."

"I know, master," and Krambambuli lay down, his head pressed close to his outstretched paws, and looked at the ranger.

Yes—if the wretched brute had not looked at him! He might have made a quick end of it all, and saved himself and the dog further pain. But he could not. Who could shoot a creature that looked at him like that! Hopp muttered a few curses between his clenched teeth, each one more lurid than the last—bent over the poacher's body, took the hares, and went on his way.

The dog followed him with his eyes until he had disappeared among the trees; then he rose to his feet, and a blood-curdling howl rang through the woods. He went round a few times in an aimless circle, and then sat down again by the dead man. In that position the officers of justice found him, when, led by Hopp, at nightfall they came to view the body and provide for its removal. Krambambuli drew back a few paces when the men approached. "There's your dog," said one of them to the ranger.

"I left him here to watch," answered Hopp, ashamed to confess the truth. But it was no use—the truth came out just the same; for when the corpse was put on the cart and carried away, Krambambuli trotted after it, head and tail drooping.

Next day a court attendant saw him slinking about near the room where the body of "Yellow" lay. The man gave him a kick and called out "Go home!" Krambambuli snarled at him and ran away, as the man thought, in the direction of the ranger's house. He did not go there, though, but began to lead a miserable vagabond life.

Wild, and worn to a skeleton, he wandered about the poor dwellings of the cottagers at the end of the village. Suddenly he darted on a child that was standing in front of the last house, and snatched greedily from him the crust of bread that he was munching. The child was speechless with fright, but a small Spitz dog ran out of the house and barked at the robber. Krambambuli dropped his booty and fled.

That same evening Hopp was standing at his window before going to bed, looking out into the bright summer night. In fancy he saw the dog sitting on the other side of the heath by the edge of the wood, gazing at the scene of his former happiness with unchanged longing—the truest of the true, masterless!

The ranger closed the shutters and went to bed. But after a while he got up again, went once more to the window and looked out—but the dog was not there. Again he tried to sleep, and a second time it was in vain.

He could bear it no longer. Whatever had passed, *he* could not get on without the dog. "I'll take him back!" he thought to himself, and felt himself a new man after the decision.

At the first peep of day he dressed himself, told his wife not to wait dinner for him, and hastened away. But as he left the house, he stumbled over the wanderer whom he had gone to seek afar off. Krambambuli lay dead at his feet, his head touching the threshold that he had not dared to cross.

The ranger never got over it. Those were his best hours in which he forgot that he had lost him. Deep in affectionate thought, he would murmur as of old, "How goes it with my Krambam—." But in the middle of the name he would stop suddenly, remembering, shake his head, and say with a heavy sigh—"Too bad about the old dog!"

THE DISTRICT DOCTOR

I

DOCTOR NATHANIEL ROSENZWEIG had had a youth full of privations. What enjoyment means was unknown to him in the brightest period of life. To suffer from hunger today and earn just enough to be enabled to go on suffering from hunger tomorrow; at two o'clock in the morning to curl himself up like a hedgehog in a corner of the underground room to sleep the dreamless sleep of exhaustion; to be roused by the whining of his old grandmother, who excused herself for being still on earth and for having to be a burden to him; to hurry away to teach in order to attain the possibility of learning himself — this was the course of his life year in, year out. To acquire was the essence of all his thoughts and dreams; to acquire money, knowledge, favor, particularly that of his professors (Nathaniel studied medicine at the University of Cracow); to acquire at any cost save only at the cost of honesty; to acquire and be sure to expend nothing without return, not even the least bit of his own strength; to be unmoved by any sympathetic impulse, any considerations that would retard his progress.

His grandmother and himself, himself and his grandmother, constituted his world, and as his world was small, so were his aims narrow. The first and most difficult achievement was to save enough money to keep himself and the old woman from starving, should some unforeseen stroke of fate incapacitate him for a time. When he had accomplished that he felt as if he was a capitalist, and consoled his grandmother when uttering her daily morning lamentation, with:

"Just go on living in peace; it is not likely that anything bad can happen to us now."

His indefatigable diligence was not lessened after his first success; it increased, on the contrary, with his added strength.

Nathaniel grew up to be a strong man; his spider-like extremities developed into muscular arms and legs, his chest expanded, his figure, despite its spareness, acquired a certain sturdiness. His bearing was so confident, his glance so calm and clear, his speech so decided, that even his first patients — people of very low degree — would say:

"What a clever gentleman our doctor is!"

No one realized how young he was: he had consorted too long with care, and even though he had mastered and conquered it he could not prevent its continuing to gnaw at him secretly.

Gradually he acquired a reputation, modest but favorable, and it was owing to it that he was at the early age of thirty appointed to the position of district physician in the western part of the province. A sure means of livelihood henceforth — ample, too, according to Nathaniel's notions. He need not have been so painfully close in fitting up his dwelling, in the market place of the district-capital, but he was afraid he might become puffed up with pride as most poor people do who rise to sudden wealth, and he threw but little work in the workingmen's way. Always bearing the saying in mind: "An ax in the house saves the carpenter," he provided himself with all sorts of tools, and was pleased to save the cabinet-maker and locksmith as well. And although his household furnishings were dreadful to look upon, that did not disconcert the doctor; he either lacked the esthetic sense or it was not developed.

When the grandmother, aged and unable to move about, could no longer leave her room, yet yearned for the sight of a green shrub, a flower in bloom, then the doctor became a gardener, and before long the windows of his house resembled those of a conservatory.

The old woman suffered at times from a recurrence of her former faint-heartedness, only it manifested itself now in a different form.

"If I only do not die too soon," said the nonagenarian. "A funeral costs so much!"

Nathaniel comforted her lovingly.

"Don't die, grandmother, you would defraud me of the reward for all the pains which I have taken for your sake."

Nathaniel's fortune increased apace, his joy in possession continued to grow and grow. Plans to realize which would have appeared to the prudent man in his youth a sheer impossibility, he now pondered with the confidence of impending fulfilment. His practice was extensive and remunerative. He was called to all the castles in the neighborhood. The dry, reticent Doctor Rosenzweig, who brooked no contradiction, who never allowed a flattery to pass his lips, became the confidant of noblemen, and, what was far more remarkable, the oracle of their charming, elegant wives, and the friend of their children.

"The child is very ill, but—Doctor Rosenzweig is treating him." — "I spent the whole day in mortal anxiety about my little girl—but Rosenzweig is here now."

If only Rosenzweig was there, succor was there, and should it for once not be forthcoming, why then God did not wish it to be brought by the hand of man, that was all.

Under no circumstances did his patients show themselves niggardly toward him—nobody would have dared. — Doctor Rosenzweig is building himself a house, a house of burnt brick—that takes money. He has leased a building-site outside of the city, and a square, one-story box of a house, has been put up on it under his own direction. It rests upon a solidly built cellar, is provided with stone steps and a weather-proof tiled roof. The window-frames are painted a snowy white, the walls whitewashed snow-white too. The only ornament that graces the façade is the little tablet of the life-insurance company by the side of the doorbell.

The windows of the front — it faces the east and the first story is occupied by the doctor and his grandmother — command a wide prospect — sky and fields. The eye roams unconfined into the endless distance. No hill obstructs it, no wood marks a dark spot upon the smooth surface of the plain, gleaming golden in summer, silvery in winter. Every foot of soil can be saturated by the life-giving rays of the blessed sun. If there is a shadow, it is a shadow that passes and does not chill, that robs not the tiniest blade of the warmth which it requires for its wondrously mysterious growth — the shadow of the fleeting clouds. How often does Nathaniel follow it with attentive gaze, watch it glide over the ripening, swelling abundance, which will be garnered in the autumn, shipped on the Vistula to Germany and Russia, and sold at a high price. Could one but have a share in his magnificent profit, have a hundredth, nay, only a thousandth part of the returns flow into one's own pocket! The doctor begins to build air-castles upon the boundless plain, so iridescent and fabulously beautiful that he cannot help smiling as he builds them: Dost thou call to me, too, thou unclaimed heritage of my ancestors — Oriental imagination?

He turns from the sight of others' affluence and wishes to draw a line between it and his own modest property. A neat picket fence surrounds the house at a distance of ten yards on every side; after every twenty pickets there is a strong, pointed post. In the space between house and fence a little garden will gradually come into existence; the division into flower and vegetable beds is already outlined. No chessboard can be more exactly divided.

"Next year, grandmother dear, you will see roses and

mignonette blooming under your window," Nathaniel promised the old woman, and she replied:

"If I only live to see it, my child. I shall be ninety-five my next birthday."

"Way over a hundred must you live to be!" he cried eagerly. "You owe it to me, think of that! How people's confidence would increase still more if everybody were saying, 'He has succeeded in making his grandmother live to be over a hundred years old.' For people are stupid, granny, they attribute to my skill what is due to your good constitution. Just keep up your courage and make up your mind firmly that you will not die yet. You will continue to live on cheerfully just as long as you can make up your mind to do so."

The old woman did decide to live on, but as for any real cheerfulness, that was out of the question.

"I often feel now," she would say, "as if your grandfather stepped before me and spoke to me as he did in his dying hour: 'Come soon! We shall live as peacefully in the garden of Eden as we did on earth. Follow me soon, Rebecca.' ... Then I could not obey the call of my loved one, because you kept me back, you helpless little creature, left so entirely alone. First your father and mother went and soon after your grandfather. Yes, it was a fearful pestilence which God visited upon his people in Kazimirz, and I knew not to whom to turn and say: 'Be kind to my grandchild if I, too, should lie down and die.' So I dared not then fulfil the wish of my loved one. But now, Nathaniel my child, I feel as if I ought not to keep him waiting any longer."

Such speeches cut the doctor to the heart. Never had the reserved, silent grandmother spoken in that way before. A suspicious sign when old people depart from their habits! The little changes are often succeeded but too soon by the irrevocable, the final one. And yet another symptom disturbed the doctor. The old woman, who formerly could never have enough solitude, now no longer liked to remain alone. Every time Nathaniel bade her good-by she would say:

"Go, in God's name, but send me the 'Goi'* to keep me company, so that I can look at a human face and not only and always at the fields and the sky."

The "Goi" was a youth of eighteen, the doctor's famulus, his servant, his slave. He could not remember a time when his "benefactor" had vouchsafed him a kind word or presented him with a good article of clothing. When Rosenzweig's coats and boots could no longer be used, they would be given to the tall young fellow, with the admonition that they should be treated with the care due to other people's property. The doctor steadily expanded in breadth, and it almost seemed as if he diminished in height. His famulus grew more and more "attenuated," as Doctor Rosenzweig expressed it, every day, and shot up, asparagus like, into the air. The way the benefactor's clothes sat upon him struck the former himself as either pitiful or ridiculous — both with an admixture of contempt.

He simply could not bear the youth, his antipathy was insurmountable and sprang from the thought that the foundling was eating his master's bread gratuitously or nearly so.

Four years since Rosenzweig had picked him up from the street, upon an icy, splendid winter night. With the pride of a triumphant hero, the doctor was spinning along swift as an arrow in the sledge of Count W. At his departure the Count himself had wrapped him carefully in the fur cover which felt so comfortable, had thanked him again and again, and sought over and over for new words to express the inexpressible — the bliss of a loving heart to whom what is dearest, what he had considered

---

* Gentile.

as lost, has been restored. Saved was the young Countess, saved from almost certain death by the genius, the resourceful care of the incomparable physician, who stood at her bedside like a hero on the field of battle, almost vanquished, yet with victory in his eye, ready for combat even while succumbing; who had not budged until he could say:

"We have won the day, she will live!"

He had watched so many nights that he looked forward to the refreshing sleep on his journey home in the comfortable sledge. But his fatigue must have been too great, it banished the longed-for refreshment instead of inducing it. As often as Nathaniel would close his eyes they would open involuntarily and revel in the sight of the star-gemmed moon-lit heavens and the snow-covered plain, which glistened with a wonderful brilliance, like some huge fresh-minted silver coin. ... How much gold could be had for such a coin? The vaults of his quadrangular dwelling would not have room to contain them, the precious, the adorable ingots! Harborer and bearer of all-conquering forces, latent witchery, garnered power. What cannot be got in exchange for gold? Treasures beyond price are purchased with it—that the man knows who restores the health of those who pay him.

The doctor's flight of thought was suddenly interrupted. The vehicle stopped close to the ditch, and the driver cried:

"Doctor! doctor!"

"What is it, my son?"

"Doctor, two drunken people are lying out there."

"Get down and give them a drubbing so that they won't freeze."

While the driver was dismounting and fastening the reins to his seat, Nathaniel had risen and bent forward, and was gazing with strained attention at the face, brightly illumined by the moon, of one of the figures lying on the ground. No drunkard's face, surely! but one that gave evidence of downright want, and suffering to the limit of human endurance.

The poor devil had, at least at the moment, no consciousness of misery; he seemed to be sound asleep. But when the driver took hold of him and dragged him up, he fell back at once, stiff as a block of ice, into the snow. The driver said:

"Doctor, one of them is already frozen."

Rosenzweig jumped from the carriage and soon convinced himself that the driver's assertion was correct. He was filled with rage. Here again he had been forestalled by death, the kind of death he hated most — not death caused by sickness or old age, hut death brought about by chance, a death which gets its prey gratuitously, gaining possession foolishly, absurdly, without any sound reason.

"Let us look after the other one," muttered the doctor between his teeth.

The other was sleeping, too, but not so profoundly.

It was a boy of about fourteen years, evidently closely related to the deceased — his brother, younger by many years, or his son.

With professional ardor the doctor essayed various means of restoration, and after long effort they were crowned with moderate success. A scarcely perceptible trickling coursed through the boy's rigid arteries, and though it ceased almost immediately, the doctor nevertheless declared with victorious assurance:

"I have him now!"

And wrapping the boy in his fur, he lifted him into the sledge, took him home and laid him in his own bed, where he watched over the child of misfortune with the same devotion that he had shown to the Countess in the castle. Next morning the patient was out of danger, and Rosenzweig could not refrain from remarking to himself: "This one, also, saved — two between two risings of the sun!"

He stroked his long, patriarchal beard complacently and rejoiced in his wonderful ability.

But he said to his patient that very day:

"Get up and go."

"Where, doctor, where? Who will take me without my brother," the boy rejoined despairingly; and now the question arose: What to do with him?

The papers found on the person of the deceased showed him to have been a machinist, Julian Mierski by name, who had for many years served as foreman in a factory in Lemberg. In his certificate of character it was stated that his employer was, to his regret, compelled to discharge this excellent workman on account of a severe illness. Since that time he had been unable to make any money, and only very little could be earned by his brother, whom he had taken care of upon the death of their parents — poor cottagers — in a village near Lemberg. Thus, the boy related, the savings of years were used up in a few months, with the exception of some florins, whose exact amount he indicated, and which had actually been found in the dead man's wallet.

The grandmother listened attentively to the lad's tearful account.

"Listen, Nathaniel, my child," said she. "It was not right of that Goi in Lemberg to forsake in his sickness the man who had served him in health so many years."

"A factory is not a charitable institution," rejoined Rosenzweig, and he bade the lad proceed.

The boy continued:

"A week ago an acquaintance of my brother called and told us that there was a factory in Cracow like ours, and that we would surely find work there. My brother was very glad: 'Come, Joseph, let us set out,' he said; and on the journey he would keep saying that it was his long idleness that had prevented him from getting well, that walking was doing him good. But all of a sudden he could go no further and lay down in the snow in order to sleep a while."

"And you allowed that?" the doctor shouted at him. "Don't you know what happens to a person in such bitter cold weather if he lies down in the snow?"

The boy lowered his big eyes, which were still streaming with tears, and remained silent.

"What can one do with such a *chamer?*"* asked Rosenzweig addressing his grandmother.

The old woman replied:

"Let him rest yet another day under your roof. Be merciful to him. He is an orphan like you."

The following day her advice was:

"Keep him. Our maid is growing old and feeble and could make use of some help. Keep him and train him to your service. Who will blame a great man like you for having an assistant?"

Thus the foundling became an inmate of the doctor's home, and although Doctor Rosenzweig would not admit it, an exceedingly useful one. In the eyes of his master Joseph remained a "chamer," who did not gain any knowledge from books, and never could. At eighteen years of age he still found it difficult to read the simplest children's stories. After the first months, the doctor had abandoned the idea of compelling him to go to school, because it was only by corporal punishment that he could get him to attend, and his benefactor did not always find time to administer it. His mechanical aptitude, on the other hand, was great, and great his assiduity in applying it. He, too, dabbled in all trades but with better success than the doctor had done.

In everything that he undertook he displayed a skill,

* Jackass.

a facility, nay, even a taste, which proved as serviceable to the doctor's pill-boxes as they were to the flower-beds in the little garden before the house. It was always with displeasure that Nathaniel heard him praised, "the idler who knows nothing and never will know anything but how to play."

Once when he gave vent to his usual reproach, Joseph remarked:

"If you could make up your mind to take your fields under your own management, I would prove to you that I am no idler."

The doctor, flying into a passion, cried:

"My fields—what are you talking about? Don't you know that I am a Jew, and as such may not own any landed property? Don't you know that even my house is built on other people's land?"

Joseph flushed crimson with embarrassment, yet he gazed confidingly and openly into the doctor's face as he replied:

"You bought the fields in the name of Theophil von Kamatzki, but they are yours anyway."

"Tell me, boy, where did you get that information?" asked Rosenzweig, and the gesture with which he began to flourish his cane was most threatening.

Calmly Joseph returned:

"It is no secret. All the people know it and they do not begrudge you the fields."

During this colloquy they were standing in the middle of the path which, leading from the street-door to the little garden-gate, ran straight down between two beds of roses neatly bordered by mignonette. On the gooseberry hedges which Joseph had trained along the wooden paling, the first fruits were ripening. All that could be seen of delicately unfolded lettuce plants, turnips with their showy tufts, cauliflowers gleaming yellow among their curly leaves, fresh onion-shoots with their martial-looking helmets, graceful marjoram, and — *dulci cum utile* — as a boundary to every vegetable square, the sweet-scented lavender, whose tiny buds were beginning to swell — all was so exuberant with strength and health that the sight made one's heart, particularly a physician's heart, leap for joy in one's bosom. With a secret satisfaction Rosenzweig contemplated the pleasant gifts of Heaven, and said:

"Because you are a passable gardener you imagine you could be a farmer, too." He wanted to stop there but changed his mind and added, while he dug the end of his cane with great persistence into the ground and apparently followed the operation with great attention:

"I should not have obtained possession of the fields — somewhat wrongfully, I admit — had I not had reason to hope that I should soon be able to own them with good right. I suppose you know that a change is about to be made in the laws of the land, and that the Jews are also to share in the greater degree of freedom which will be given the people of Galicia."

Joseph was aware of that and hoped that the doctor, after the fields were his property before God and man, would no longer lease them but cultivate them himself.

"Then you will have to build stables and barns," the boy concluded. "I learned something by watching the architects in the city and have the plans ready."

"You are a young fool," returned the doctor — yet a few days later he asked to see the plans.

Well, practicable they certainly were not; still it must be conceded that it was remarkable that a foundling whose handwriting was like that of a child of seven should have been able to draft a plan so neat and exact, and correct, too, it may be, in its measurements. He was just one of those who can dance before they have learned to walk. There are such odd fish. They do, to be sure, strike us at times with astonishment; but as a rule they do not turn out to be anything.

Nathaniel, who never pursued a thought which concerned his weal or woe any length of time without making a confidante of his grandmother, questioned her soon after as to what she thought about his managing his estate himself. Then it appeared that that subject had already been discussed between the old woman and the foundling.

"You will grow rich like Laban," she prophesied. "The visible blessing of the Lord is upon you."

This was proved that spring, the spring of 1845, so disastrous to thousands, when the Vistula, overflowing its banks, converted the luxuriant, promisingly ripening crops into a slimy sea. Irresistible as a judgment of God, the tide had surged in, washed away the nurturing soil and with it the property and the hopes of those who cultivated it.

Close up to the boundary of Nathaniel's fields did the devastation extend—before them the waves retreated. Before them the waters had gone back and had divided, as did the waters of the Red Sea when Moses lifted his rod and stretched out his hand at God's command.

And when autumn came, famine reigned round about. Hundreds forsook their homes with their wives and children and wandered about as beggars, as day-laborers, seeking bread and work.

But the grandmother would ask every day:

"When does the harvest begin? This year wheat is worth a hundred times its usual value. When are the reapers coming?"

"Soon, very soon. They are already sharpening their scythes," Nathaniel answered smiling.

The old woman did not, however, live to see the harvest-time. She herself fell back, like overripe grain, into the lap of mother earth before her grandson could say to her:

"The reapers are coming!"

Very late and yet too soon had her life been suddenly extinguished.

There she lay, then, in her narrow coffin, old Rebecca — a strangely poignant picture. Death had straightened her bent form, and, weeping and astonished, Joseph asked:

"Was she as tall as that?"

But he likewise asked:

"Was she as beautiful as that?"

Released from all infirmities, freed from the helplessness of age, how majestic she appeared now in her everlasting rest, in a peace that naught could disturb! The smile seen on the countenances of so many who have conquered, did not hover on her lips. A stony coldness spoke from her features, which had been illumined even in her dying hour by the inspired love and admiration which the presence of her grandson had always called up.

"It is no longer you!" meditated Nathaniel, and the consciousness of his loss seized him with a terrible force.

He motioned to Joseph to leave, he wished to be alone with his dead. Standing at the foot of the bier, he strove to see in his grandmother's strange, altered countenance the one that had so long been familiar and dear to him, and he found it not. The only ideal good that he had possessed, the affection of that old woman, was gone forever, and there he was, a man getting on in years — alone. With a sudden shock the thought flashed upon him: Between you and this old woman there lies a generation. You should now be able to go and weep for her upon your wife's breast and gather consolation from the sight of your children.

The restlessly striving man who had only looked forward, never backward toward aims which grew with his successes, paused for once in his course, faced about and traversed in spirit the whole of his life's pathway. I have achieved much, he might have said to himself, but never the slightest bit without a thought of you, grandmother. She had been the source of all the brightness and happiness of his life and the void that her death had created yawned all the more painfully before him.

She should not have forsaken him, she whose presence had deceived him as to the flight of time — the sense of which is lost by the very old.

"Do not follow the custom of our people," the old woman would often say. "Do not marry too young and bring beggars into the world. You can wait, my child, you are young."

He had always remained silent at this admonition; today he answered her who could no longer hear him:

"You kept on thinking me too young to be a lover, until at last I got too old to be one."

The reproach which he had addressed to her in her coffin he felt immediately, however, to be a sacrilege. Stepping up to her, he bent over her and, what had never happened while she was alive, he kissed her hand, kissed her brow and the lips forever silent, the only ones on earth from which he had ever heard the words "my child."

II

Joseph took part in the activities of the harvest of his own accord, and one afternoon Rosenzweig, sauntering past indifferently, as if the thing did not concern him, saw him standing aloft on a pretty well-filled harvest wagon. Nimbly and energetically he was stacking the sheaves, and it struck the doctor that the lad in the queer, wide jacket which had served his benefactor as a coat, and the trousers so much too short for him, was nevertheless a remarkably handsome fellow. Tall, slim and vigorous, his countenance white and red, his well-shaped head crowned with fair, wavy hair, his whole being breathing joy in his work, in labor — he looked uncommonly well on his proud eminence.

Among the women and girls engaged in the field was the daughter of the farmer to whom Rosenzweig had leased Squire Theophil von Kamatzki's land. A pretty, lively creature — a genuine daughter of Masovia. Rosenzweig observed that the brown, sparkling eyes of the girl and the blue eyes of the lad exchanged glances quite often, and if then the brown ones were lowered in confusion they were obstinately pursued by the blue ones — so obstinately, so boldly, that they were finally compelled to be lifted, whether she wished it or not.

The disdain with which Rosenzweig regarded Joseph received new nourishment from this little incident. A fellow condemned to lasting servitude by the miserable nature of his brain, undertakes to turn that of a girl? And at what age! A mere boy, of the age which the doctor's son would be had the doctor married at the proper time. What he in heroic self-denial had delayed to achieve until he had missed the chance of achieving it, the happiness of love, this a crude, penniless fellow, dependent upon others' favors, aspired to with thoughtless levity!

That evening Rosenzweig summoned Joseph to his room. It was such a bare, cheerless-looking apartment that every one shivered who entered it — even in the dog-days. The furniture consisted of a number of chairs ranged along the wall, a huge writing-desk painted white, and a long, low bookcase, likewise painted white, which, like a counter in a shop, divided the room into two parts. The smaller one, near the windows, was appropriated by the doctor, the larger one was where the patients waited until he stepped up to them through a narrow space which had been left open between the wall and the bookcase. Upon its topmost shelf lay or stood all sorts of objects, in gruesome contemplation of which the people beguiled the time while waiting. Peculiar looking instruments, knives and forceps and tightly closed glasses filled with a transparent liquid, which the Galician instinct at once suspected to be spirits. Only, unfortunately, the good beverage was spoiled by the highly unappetizing formations swimming in it.

Across all these things Rosenzweig now called to Joseph, who had just entered:

"Now tell me what is going on between you and the farmer's daughter, Lubienka?"

As usual when his benefactor addressed him sharply, the lad turned fiery red, nor did he at once find a reply. It was only after Rosenzweig had repeated his question that he summoned up courage and answered in a low but firm tone:

"I love her."

"And she?"

"She loves me, too."

The doctor broke into a bitter, mocking laugh.

"You imagine so?"

"I know it, sir—"

"And where is this love-making to lead?"

Now, Joseph thought the doctor was making sport of him, that he just wished to twit him a little, and he answered quite cheerfully:

"To marriage, sir."

"Marriage! You are thinking of marriage?"

"Yes, sir! And Lubienka is thinking of it, too."

"She, too. ... What does her father say to that?"

"He finds it all right, Panie Kochanku!"* cried Joseph with an outburst of overflowing emotion, and he looked as if he were about to rush into his benefactor's domain, forbidden to all save the doctor.

---

* Dear sir.

The latter, however, rose commandingly from his seat and calling to the lad sternly, "Stay where you are!" fixed him to the spot.

In cruel words he laid before him his poverty and his hopeless future. He was indignant at the thought that this fellow had perhaps reckoned upon him, or upon his purse, and he made up his mind to show the interested rascal the door when the work of the harvest should be completed. Meanwhile, he ordered him from the room and retired to rest with the resolve to admonish the farmer the following day to put an end to the love-making between his daughter and Joseph.

Precisely upon that day, however, something occurred which once for all drove every unessential and secondary consideration out of his mind.

Summoned early in the morning by the proprietress of a neighboring estate to the bedside of her son, who had suddenly been taken ill, he was able to reassure the anxious mother regarding the condition of the patient, and would have been glad to go home at once. The hospitable custom of the country forbade that, however. Willingly or unwillingly, he had to partake of an ample breakfast which was served in the drawing-room. A large number of guests stopping at the castle had gathered there—a company well known to the doctor, and as repellent to him as if it had consisted entirely of quacks. Adherents, of both sexes, of "King" Adam Czartoryski, conspirators against the existing order, fanatics for the restoration of the old Polish regime. The lady of the house, still young, handsome, enthusiastic, and since the death of her husband, absolute mistress of the great estate which had been her dowry, was the soul of the party and its powerful support. She kept up a lively correspondence with the national Government in Paris, received and harbored its emissaries, and expended great sums annually upon revolutionary objects.

This fanatical agitation displeased the doctor and distorted the image of the woman so estimable in every other respect—as a good mother, a clever manager of her property, a humane mistress of her subordinates.

With an expression of annoyance he took his seat at the tea-table, ate and drank, and did not utter a word, while the ladies and gentlemen were eagerly discussing politics. It seemed to him as if he were surrounded by children who, instead of playing soldiers, were, for a change, playing conspirators.

Suddenly a fair hand was laid on the arm of his chair.

"Why so dejected, dear doctor, in face of the most beautiful miracle?" said Countess Aniela W. to the man who had saved her life.

Rosenzweig arose and bowed:

"What miracle does your ladyship mean?"

"That of the revival of the Polish Kingdom!" replied the charming woman, and her dove-like eyes flashed an eagle glance, while she raised her graceful figure proudly to its full height.

The doctor suppressed a smile, and a number of patriotic ladies exclaimed in pained disappointment:

"You doubt? Oh, doctor—is it possible? A man so clever!"

"I do not doubt, ladies. Who says that I doubt!"

"Your smile—entirely groundless, since we are in earnest—says so," rejoined the Countess, and folded her arms like Napoleon.

"The moment to shake off the foreign yoke is here. You may be informed of it because you are a good Pole and our confidential friend. The signal for the outbreak of the revolution will be given in Lemberg at the archduke's opening ball!"

A general silence followed this open declaration. The conspirators were dismayed at the arbitrariness with which Aniela disposed of the common property — the plan of the party. Yet she was far too lovable and, besides, looked far too charming to permit of any feeling of resentment against her. She wore a little Parisian cap with a cascade of patriotic red and white ribbons. The rich material of her morning gown had been brought to her from Nijni-Novgorod by her husband at the time of his last mission to Russia — a feat attended with great danger.

Oh, there was quite a history connected with it ... But it was not to be related today; surely not at this moment where the main thing was to efface the unfavorable impression which the Countess, in her role as a politician, had produced upon the company.

"You people of little faith!" she exclaimed, "do you doubt the loyalty and trustworthiness of a man who has saved my life for my country?"

Several young men hastened to protest, and an old man, of the petty nobility, with a long, drooping mustache, raised his glass of Madeira, emptied it in one draught, and cried:

"Vivat Doctor Rosenzweig!"

The hostess repeated:

"Vivat Doctor Rosenzweig, to whom so many of us are indebted for our own health and that of our children!"

After this toast she gulped down the remainder of her sixth cup of tea. Instead of showing himself grateful, the doctor muttered:

"How often have I told your ladyship not to drink so much tea? You ruin your nerves."

The beautiful hostess answered with a superior smile:

"Good Heavens, my nerves! Quite different demands will soon be made upon them!"

"I understand — at that revolutionary ball!"

"Yes, doctor! Yes!" interrupted Countess Aniela — "the ball where we shall inaugurate an event of world-historic significance!"

"At the mazurka or the franchise?"

"The cotillion. The ladies choose, simultaneously, all the officers present. The officers divest themselves of their sabers for the dance. The sabers are removed. No sooner is that done than the Poles rush at the defenseless foe and cut them down!"

"Vivat!" cried the old nobleman, who had spoken before, "down with them all, no quarter!"

Some of the ladies protested, and suggested giving quarter to those officers who should ask for it. They withdrew their proposal, however, upon noticing that it excited doubts as to the genuineness of their patriotism.

"Ladies and gentlemen," said Rosenzweig, "this plan is wonderfully conceived, but as to carrying it out, you will not do it."

"Why?" was heard from all sides, "what is to hinder us?"

"Your own nobility of soul, your own loyal nature. Noble women and noble men like you may hate, may fight, but they do not betray and they do not murder."

"Monsieur," said a youth of nineteen who had just returned from a Paris educational institute, "your argument would be valid in war, but it does not apply in a conspiracy."

"Quite right — because ..." It suddenly occurred to the old noble that it was in order now for him to make a speech; jumping up and clicking his heels together, he cried, after some deliberation:

"Vivat Polonia! Vivat King Adam!"

And now a trembling, hollow voice was heard issuing from a corner of the room. It seemed as if it proceeded from the depths of a mountain — a mountain of silk, soft draperies, laces, ruffles, and ribbons. The voice belonged to Sulpicia, wife of the Starost,* great-aunt of the hostess, in whose house the old lady lived, enjoying a most bounteous charity.

"Olga, Duschenka moja,"** said she, "think above all of your eternal salvation."

The hostess had noticed with consternation the gradual decline of the enthusiasm of her guests, while she herself, after her seventh cup of tea, had attained the highest summit of inspiration. The old lady had with her admonition poured oil upon the fire. It blazed forth at once, too, in the resounding, solemn cry:

"All for Poland! My earthly and my eternal salvation!"

Countess Aniela, quite transported by this loftiness of spirit, threw herself into her friend's arms, the gentlemen kissed the hands of the fair patriots. One of them requested the honor of drinking from the hostess' slipper. She would not permit it, however, out of regard for the exalted earnestness of the hour, and the one whose plea had been rejected seated himself at the piano and struck up a plaintive national melody.

All remained silent, all listened with emotion, many eyes were dim with tears.

The irresistible power of the song affected even one who up to that time had stood impassive in the embrasure of a window and taken no part in the conversation.

Rosenzweig did not know him and, with his innate distrust, was inclined to take him, on account of his striking pallor, for one of those diffident patients who are so glad to put themselves in the way of famous physicians on neutral ground, in order, incidentally, to get their advice, for which they omit to pay a fee.

---

* A nobleman, owner of a castle or domain called a Starosty.
** My darling.

However, Rosenzweig was mistaken. The stranger made no attempt to approach him, while on the contrary the doctor could not disengage his attention from the stranger.

He was a man of medium height, slender, with a fair, scant beard, with blue and evidently very near-sighted eyes. The impression of great spiritual activity produced by his features was heightened by the pallor which had at first misled the doctor into thinking him an invalid. But he soon changed his mind on that point, too. Ill health does not spiritualize, as the poets often assert; it marks the children of the earth rather with distinct tokens of their origin.

In the appearance of this man, however, no signs of bodily distress were visible. The traces of suffering on his marble-like brow had been stamped there by restless working thoughts, and the lines round the youthful lips by early and strenuous spiritual conflicts. The disdain with which the doings of the company seemed to inspire him had been gradually overcome. The strains of the beautiful national air touched and thrilled him too. One emotion bound him to his brethren — longing, a passionately fervent longing for his lost fatherland.

Of this fount of suffering no people has drunk so deep as the one from whose heart this song has gushed. It sings of the prodigal son who returns to his parental home filled with repentance and glowing love. Halting he stands at the closed door and hears the voice of his father, who calls to him, and hears the weeping of his mother. ... "Father! Mother!" he groans. They answer: "Come, deliver us, we are lying in chains." ... He rattles at the iron gate, wounds his hands with knocking, bruises his brow, the blood begins to flow. In vain. Never will that gate yield, never will he be able to unhinge it. He will perish on the threshold.

The song ceased, and the silence that followed it

was only broken after a space by the hostess, who rose, went up to the stranger and conferred with him in a low voice.

The stately lady seemed literally to make herself small before her guest, her whole attitude attesting veneration, all her gestures, homage.

Folding her hands, she exclaimed imploringly:

"Speak, oh speak to the assembly!"

The appeal of the hostess received enthusiastic support.

"Oh yes, speak!" cried many voices in unison. — "It would give us new courage." — "We have only been waiting to get the courage to ask you." — "Modesty forbade."

All of them approached, with friendliest mien, with punctilious courtesy — none without a certain awe. Even the triumphant Countess Aniela was constrained, and her lovely lips were tremulous as she said:

"Give us a proof of your marvelous eloquence, of which we have heard so much. It is said that you are capable of moving hearts of stone and rousing the morally dead to the noblest deeds!"

The stranger laughed, and his laugh was as clear and fresh as that of a child. Involuntarily Rosenzweig was forced to think: You have an innocent soul.

"What is his name?" he asked his hostess.

She blushed and replied with a rather unsuccessfully assumed indifference:

"It is my cousin Roswadowski, from the Kingdom."*

The doctor had never heard of any famous orator named Roswadowski; but what did that signify? In times of national revolt national notabilities spring up over night.

---

* Part of Russian Poland. (The Congress of Vienna in 1815 converted most of the Duchy of Warsaw into the so-called Kingdom of Poland, ruled by the Russian tsar - A.M.)

Roswadowski returned the look which the doctor fixed upon him with one equally searching, and, with a slight inclination of his head toward him, said:

"Why not ask Doctor Rosenzweig to speak? He might tell you what he expects from the revolution."

"We know that in advance," rejoined Aniela, "like every good Pole, the restoration of the kingdom, the general welfare."

"Olga, Duschenka moja," again the great-aunt let herself be heard, "tell your friend Aniela that no one is a good Pole who is not a good Catholic."

Without taking heed of the interruption, Roswadowski pursued:

"The general welfare should embrace every individual interest, consequently that of this man and his co-religionists as well. Why do I not hear any of you who are so full of his praise say that you purpose to pay the debt which we all owe to him and his people?"

"*Ce cher Eduard!*" exclaimed Count W., and, swaying his body and smiling suavely, he added, in a voice audible only to his wife and to Rosenzweig, who was standing near her: "He is growing madder every day."

The hostess, too, was dissatisfied with her cousin's unexpected outburst, and declared very sharply that she on her part, at least, did not feel as if she owed a debt of gratitude and reverence to the excellent physician.

"And as regards the equal rights of all creeds in the Polish Kingdom," observed Aniela, "it is already established in principle. The modes of procedure will be considered later. Up to this time, however, time has been lacking to enter into details."

"I prostrate myself at your feet!" exclaimed Rosenzweig. "I no longer feel any concern now for the cause of the Jews."

"Your promise arouses his mirth, so great is his confidence" — Roswadowski put in. "He whose whole life consists in the devoted performance of his duty toward us expects from us—nothing."

"Sir, if I did not do my duty, I should forfeit my position," the doctor interposed, in the tone of a man who wishes to put an end to a disagreeable discussion.

His unbidden advocate rejoined, however:

"When I spoke of duty I had a higher one in mind than the one imposed on you by your office. Officially you are an able district-physician—it is your own heart that makes you a Samaritan."

"A Samaritan! ... I?"

"Yes, you! The one in the Gospel cared for the dying man on the highway and then gave him over to the care of others. The dying man whom *you* found on your path you received in your house, which has become a home for the orphaned Christian boy."

The doctor replied disparagingly:

"Just as one chooses to look at it," and thought to himself grimly: "You are well informed, you flatterer! My house a home for such a *chanter!*"

And at that moment he obtained the answer to a question which he had often pondered—whether a person can think of two things at once; for, in good truth, he was thinking at the same time: Before sending away the *chanter* I shall have a new suit made for him.

"Thus acted a Jew," said the orator, turning to the company, "of his own free will, toward one of a different faith, and what have we of a different faith ever voluntarily done for one of his race? Read your history and ask yourselves whether a Jew *can* wish for the day when Poles shall again govern Poland."

Olga and Aniela remonstrated; as for the gentlemen, most of them had followed Count W. into the adjoining room and seated themselves at the card-table. The venerable noble and the new arrival from Paris alone remained chivalrously with the ladies, the former declaring that he, too, had in his youth occupied himself with the history of his country, but had never read of aught but glorious deeds.

Now the door was flung open, and a servant rushed in and cried:

"The prefect of the district. He will soon drive into the courtyard."

The brave women uttered a cry of horror:

"Great Heavens! The prefect!"

In mortal anxiety the hostess grasped her cousin's hand. "Away, away, hide yourself!"

"I am not thinking of it," returned he quite calmly, "I am very glad to make the acquaintance of so amiable a gentleman."

"You shall not stay! You must go — because your presence compromises us," exclaimed Count W., who, with consternation in his face, had returned to the salon.

An altercation ensued.

"Doctor, I beseech you, hasten to meet the prefect, try to detain him as long as possible on the steps," implored the mistress of the mansion, and hurried Rosenzweig to the door.

"I shall do what I can; I bid you good-by, ladies and gentlemen!" he answered, and left the salon, highly delighted in the bottom of his heart at the turn which the gathering of the conspirators had taken.

From the hall he saw the prefect just entering the house. A portly, elegant-looking man, dressed with the utmost care. The top of his silk hat glistened, in the glimpse which the doctor first had of it, like the moon's disk. No less shone the patent-leather boot on the little foot which he set on the lowest step as Rosenzweig reached him.

"I have the pleasure of welcoming your Honor," said the doctor, flourishing his hat ceremoniously.

"My dear doctor? Is it really you? What?" the official

responded, with a most gracious smile, "you, too, in the nest of the conspirators?"

"Dropped out like a little unfledged bird! — How fares your Honor?"

"Well. Thanks to your directions."

"And the exactness with which your Honor follows them. You are such an excellent patient that you deserve to be sick all the time."

"Greatly obliged for the Christian wish ... Pardon me — it was a slip of the tongue." And now came the question which the prefect never spared the doctor even at a most cursory meeting. "But, my dear doctor, when will you at last be baptized?"

The standing question received the standing answer:

"I don't yet know exactly."

"Make up your mind! You are anyway only half a Jew."

"I should presumably be likewise only half a Christian."

"Oh! that is a different matter!" rejoined the official, severely. "We are not talking of that; now tell me — " his expression remained unchanged, but his small, shrewd eyes cast a penetrating glance at the physician: "Is he upstairs, the emissary? Have you seen him?"

"What emissary?"

"In this house he is introduced as Herr von Roswadowski."

An expression of such honest astonishment was pictured on the doctor's countenance, that the official explained:

"You are not initiated! — Well, I shall not rob you of your political innocence. ... Quite charming, those conspirators! particularly the ladies. For that matter, there is less reason for us to beware of them than for them to beware — of others. There is a storm brewing over their heads of which they haven't the faintest suspicion.

These harmless malcontents, who consider themselves dangerous, are themselves threatened by persons discontented from quite different causes and dangerous in quite a different way."

Rosenzweig had no time to ask for an explanation, for the mistress of the mansion, beaming with friendliness, appeared at the head of the stairway, and the prefect advanced to meet her with graceful, rapid steps.

III

Rosenzweig sent word to his coachman to harness up and follow him. He himself started ahead on foot and soon struck a narrow path, which, crossing the field obliquely, led close to a stone cross on the highway. He intended to wait there for his carriage.

He longed to take good long strides, breathe the fresh, free air, inhale the wholesome odor which rose from the ploughed-up earth. But he wondered why he did not experience a keener sense of joy and satisfaction at having escaped from the perfumed atmosphere of the salon.

A feeling of profound discomfort took possession of him, a vague emotion which he could not account for but which troubled him greatly.

Suddenly he cried out loud and repeatedly: "Fool! Fool!"

The apostrophe was intended for the person whom the prefect had termed an emissary, and it was the recollection of the unmerited praise which the fellow had bestowed on him that put the doctor out of humor. Every word that the "fool" had uttered, every trait of his spiritual apostle's face, the expression of rapturous veneration with which his deep-blue eyes had rested upon him—he heard all, he saw all again, and it filled him with wrathful shame.

He, the dry Nathaniel Rosenzweig, intent upon his own advantage, a philanthropist and Samaritan? Alone as he was here in the field, the blood surged to his cheeks in a fiery glow. He recalled the hands which in the course of his long life had been stretched out to him in supplication, and said to himself: "Never have you given help except professionally. And what we do in that way, we do for our own sake." His duty he had done fully; but duty — the word itself implies it — is only an exchange. More than this he had never done — he had given his energy, his talent, the fruits of his steadily increasing knowledge, in exchange for the prosperity and the esteem which he gained through them. Thus had he hitherto acted and — he threw back his head on his stout shoulders — thus he meant to act in the future. Let every one first follow his example; let this degree of morality, though essentially a low one, first be attained by the majority of mankind, then may the idealists, the dreamers of a golden age of universal brotherhood have their say — not before!

Now he was himself again, and strode on firmly and cheerfully, in his usual calm spirit.

Long before his carriage, of which he could not catch a glimpse, though he looked hard, he reached the stone cross. At its foot there cowered a pitiful figure. An old man, his knees drawn up to his chin, a high sheepskin cap on his head, about his shoulders the remnants of a blue dress-coat which the late land-owner had presumably worn in the days of slumbering patriotism. Frayed linen trousers hung about his thin legs, which, like the rest of his body, were trembling incessantly.

When the doctor approached and addressed him, he lifted his bronzed and furrowed countenance slowly and with an effort, and looked at him with his dim, red-rimmed eyes with the humble, suffering expression of an old staghound.

"What are you doing here?" demanded Rosenzweig.

"I am waiting, your Honor, I am waiting and praying," answered the old man, stretching out a bony right hand, upon which hung a much used rosary; "I am always waiting for a letter from our good Lord."

"What do you expect our good Lord to write to you?"

"That I may go to Him; it is high time, very high time."

"How old are you?"

"Seventy, no more. But see how I look, and if your Honor knew how I feel. Here " —and he tapped upon his hollow, wheezy chest—"no breath. Every day I think I shall die on the way, that I shall not reach the cross."

"Why don't you stay at home?"

The old man stretched out his arms with an indescribably forlorn gesture. "They drive me out, my daughter, my son-in-law, the children. Well, yes—they have no room themselves in the little hovel."

"To whom does the hovel belong?"

"To my daughter. Yes, my daughter. I made her a present of it for her dowry."

"A petticoat-property, then!" scoffed the doctor. "And now she drives you out of the house that you gave her?"

"Great Heaven, what shall she do? My son-in-law beats her because I live so long. He tells the children: 'Children, pray that your grandfather may die soon' —Yes."

"You have a fine son-in-law."

"Good Lord, sir, people are that way. Gentlemen like you don't know how people are. There are others in the village who are much worse. Particularly at this time." He lowered his wheezy voice. "Woe to all the *panowies* and *panies** who live to see the coming year!"

"And why? What do you mean by that?"

---

* Masters and mistresses.

"Oh the poor gentry! The poor, poor things!" whined the old man, and began to cry bitterly. "Everything will be taken from them, and they will be murdered, too."

The doctor burst out: "You are not in your right mind!"

And now the old man, wringing his hands, cried:

"You answer me like that, too! That is a misfortune! ... The priest answered me like that when I told what I knew in the confessional; the agent answered me like that, and the bailiff even threatened to have me flogged for saying such things. ..." And turning his shifting glance upon the doctor he added: "Are you agreed with them, too?"

"Agreed—I? With whom! ... Tell me everything," commanded Rosenzweig. "What will happen the coming year!"

"People from beyond the sea will come and will divide all the property of the nobility among the peasants."

"That of Pan Theophilus Kamatzki, too. Just wait, canaille!" mused the doctor, and said: "And what will the Government say to that?"

"The Government? Oh Jesus! The Government had all the land surveyed last spring so that the foreigners may know how it should be divided."

Rosenzweig burst into a loud laugh: "Oh this people ... I have had dealings with this people for fifty years, but the ways of their folly I have not yet fathomed. ... Old man! The Emperor had the surveys made because he wants to know how large his Galicia is and how much taxes it can pay him."

The old man shook his head incredulously: "We know better, pardon me. The Emperor takes away the land from the gentry who are against him and gives it to the peasants who are for him. Then all will be well, most people think. ... I think it will be bad. Every day will be Sunday, and what do the peasants do on Sunday but fight and get drunk? ... Oh gracious sir, if it could only be prevented!"

"Set your mind at rest, it will certainly be prevented," returned Rosenzweig, laughing again.

At that the old man's ire was suddenly roused:

"If you had been at the tavern last night and had heard the commissary preach, you wouldn't laugh."

"The commissary? The emissary, I suppose you mean to say. An emissary, such as wander about now by the dozen."

"No, no, not such a one. One who was a master once and says now that there should no longer be any masters. He knows so well what is coming that he preferred to become a peasant at once of his own free will, and has given everything away."

These words aroused Nathaniel's keenest attention and convinced him that the old man was speaking of the same man whom the prefect had termed an emissary and with whom he himself had just stood face to face.

The same! it was he—he, beyond doubt, the enigmatical being the story of whose life was discussed by the sensible with scorn and derision, by the timid with hatred, by the visionary with enthusiasm; it was—*Edward Dembowski.*

Often had he heard that this man exercised a witchery which none could resist, and he had regarded this mysterious influence with the greatest incredulity; and now he admitted to himself that in reality he was experiencing a kindred sensation.

Yes, the pallid enthusiast stalked like a spectre by his side. His image pursued him with intolerable persistence. In vain did he strive to turn his thoughts from it, it emerged ever anew and defied his will to banish it.

The doctor's carriage had been standing for some time on the road. A comfortable *britzschka* with a pair of well-fed, cream-colored mares in graceful harness and collars hung with bells. The driver was a slim fellow, clad in a neat, simply braided coat; the whole formed a handsome turn-out which aroused the envy of many a nobleman.

The doctor patted the horses' stout necks and straightened the little plaits of their black manes. He was just on the point of stepping into the carriage when he turned and called to the old man at the foot of the cross:

"What is your name?"

"Semen Plachta, sir."

"Listen to me, Semen! Crawl home and tell your son-in-law that Doctor Rosenzweig is coming to visit you tomorrow. He should leave you at home. Do you understand me? If I do not find you at home when I come, I shall see to it that your son-in-law shall, even before the general distribution, receive a thrashing as the first advance payment." Rosenzweig had pulled out his purse and taken out a five-gulden note. His face grew very serious as he contemplated it. A brief hesitation — then he handed it to the old man.

"Now, this belongs to you. I want to hear tomorrow whether this money has been expended for you."

Semen stretched out his hand for the fabulous wealth — speak, think, he could not.

The driver, too, was stunned, opened his eyes wide, and almost dropped the reins from astonishment. What in Heaven's name could it mean? His master give away five gulden to a street-beggar!

"Master," said he as the doctor stepped into the carriage, "you gave him five gulden. Didn't you make a mistake?"

"Hold your tongue and drive on!" commanded Rosenzweig, and the whip cracked and the roans started up.

Soon the physician's house came into view on the broad plain. It no longer stood there quite alone like a landmark; neat-looking stables and sheds, ranged in the form of a horse-shoe, were to be seen in the background, and a carefully cultivated nursery filled the space between the dwelling and the outhouses.

The latter had, indeed, been built according to a plan of the *chanter*, which had been approved by the architect, and, it had to be admitted, had turned out well.

Whether Rosenzweig returned to his home from the farm of a petty noble, from the dwelling of the lord of a manor, or from the castle of a magnate, he always greeted his beloved possession with the same feeling of satisfaction. "Let others have what they may but give me my own!" And in reality he would not have changed with anybody, no matter how profitable the exchange. For he had never loved a living being, his grandmother excepted, as he loved his little estate. And as it lay there so trim before him, the possession so slowly and arduously acquired, an embodiment of his strength and ability, a property founded, as few are, in right and justice, he clenched his fists and dealt an imaginary murderous blow at the imaginary person who should dare to touch it.

That very evening he called on the prefect and reported to him word for word his conversation with Semen Plachta.

The official entered into a detailed discussion of the communistic plots in the country, but the real object of their originator, or the nature of that singular being, he was unable to explain, close as was his knowledge of the whole course of the man's life.

The emissary, who wandered indefatigably through the country and preached in palace and cabin the gospel of the equal rights of all mankind and of the equal division of all landed property, belonged, as a son of the Senator-Castellan of Poland and lord of the manorial estate of Rody in the government of Warsaw, to the high nobility. He, too, like the others of his class, had grown up and been trained in the consciousness of transmitted rights and inherited power, and the duty of maintaining and exercising them.

Scarcely had he obtained possession of them, however, when he voluntarily relinquished them. The revenue from his estates found its way into the poor man's wallet or was expended upon revolutionary objects. He himself wandered about recruiting disciples for his doctrines, finding them in the ranks of his own class. He appealed to the impressionable hearts of youth, and the purer and more innocent they were, the more ardent was their adoration of him, their longing to follow his self-sacrificing example. Apostles of the emissary made their appearance in the Kingdom of Poland, in western Russia, in Posen, in Galicia. With the words of their idol on their lips, they cried to the aristocracy: "Cast from you the riches and the privileges you have too long enjoyed. Privilege is injustice." And to the people: "Come, ye poor ones! Take your share of the soil which for hundreds of years you have enriched with the sweat of your brow, and — oh how often! — with your blood as well." — But to all they said: "Arise, shake off the yoke of the foreigner. We want to found a kingdom where there shall be neither superfluity nor poverty, dominion nor servitude, a kingdom such as Christ preached."

The spiritual leader of this missionary campaign had meanwhile participated in the revolt of 1843 against Russia, frustrated almost at the moment of its outbreak. He escaped to Posen as a fugitive, was called to account before long for spreading communistic principles, imprisoned, and finally banished. He repaired to Brussels, where Lelewel was paying the penalty for the aberrations of his all too ardent love of liberty and country in the torments of the bitterest homesickness. Intercourse with that "Grand Master of Revolutionaries" heightened Dembowski's enthusiasm to fanaticism. What thenceforth filled his soul was not alone sympathy with the wretched and the needy, but a hatred of the powerful and the rich, whether they were the rulers of the Powers that had partitioned Poland, or the masters of the Polish junta in Paris, usurpers of the kingdom which they wished to restore.

The apostle of brotherly love returned to his country as a political agitator. He who hitherto had followed only his own impulses undertook to carry out the plans of others, and the task of preparing the soil of Galicia for revolt. He was working now to that end. Did those who intrusted him with that mission know what they were doing? Did they look upon him and his teaching simply as a leaven which was to start the dull masses fermenting and set them moving, assuming that they themselves had the power to dictate in what direction?

The sympathy and admiration which every genuine Pole feels for one who has suffered in the struggle against foreign rule was once again attested. The aristocracy shielded the outlaw, although they recognized in him an enemy to their interests. No matter what party he belonged to, the liberation of Poland was one of his aims—they met on the way and grasped each other's hands.

"And see here," concluded the prefect, "the man in me has not been so completely merged in the official that I should not love these Poles for their patriotism, often heedless, blind, but always high-souled—yes, and envy them for it."

"Your Excellency!" exclaimed Nathaniel in a disapproving tone, and both men remained silent. It was only after a long pause that the doctor resumed:

"I believe, your Excellency, that it is, above all, the duty of the Government to protect itself and the nobility from the pernicious influence of the communistic aristocrat." Here he interjected the Ruthenian adage: "It is an evil bird that fouls its own nest." — "I cannot understand why they look on so long without taking any action; why he is not prevented from disseminating his deadly poison under the very eyes, as it were, of legal authority."

Disagreeably impressed by Rosenzweig's determined manner, the prefect replied with a cool air of superiority:

"It is hardly done without a reason. Moreover — between ourselves! — we have directions to keep track of him — in an inconspicuous manner."

"Oh — if that is the case!" cried Nathaniel with an excess of zeal, "then I implore your Excellency to make use of my services. Nothing would be more inconspicuous than to intrust a sick man to the care of a physician. And that your 'emissary' is sick — here," and he pointed to his forehead, "and that his proper place is the district-physician's examining room, I can take my oath."

The expression of the official's countenance grew steadily colder; suddenly addressing an indifferent question to the doctor, he dismissed him, warningly citing to him at the same time Talleyrand's famous saying: *"Surtout pas trop de zèle."*

The warning was fruitless. The doctor's ardor in the cause of law and order once unchained could not be held within bounds. He was anxious to communicate to others the disquiet which constantly possessed him, displayed a supreme disgust against the persistent patience that prevailed among the ruling classes, terming it criminal levity and unpardonable indifference.

His political creed might, up to this time, have been summed up in one sentence: "Our Government will be the best conceivable as soon as it condescends to grant the Jews the right to own land." Now, however, his faith in the wisdom of that Government was shaken, and he began to comport himself as its instructor and adviser. He gave the prefecture no peace; daily he would bring new and increasingly ominous reports regarding the spread of the communistic propaganda, counseling ever more urgently the adoption of energetic precautionary measures.

He had made the close acquaintance of Semen Plachta's son-in-law, and this furnished him much food for thought. He had never before occupied himself with the study of a peasant's soul. A peasant had, in his eyes, been one of the most uninteresting of bipeds covered with a human skin. Now he took one under observation, studied him carefully, even accompanied him to the tavern, entered into discussions with him, and on the third day he knew, what he had really known from the first moment, that the man was lazy, addicted to drink, and stupid. How stupid, appeared only when brandy loosened his heavy tongue; and it needed but a few questions to arrive at the conclusion that he lacked even the cardinal knowledge of the distinction between mine and thine.

The doctor drove over to see the Countess Aniela and delivered a discourse to her on the condition of the rural population. "Yes," he concluded, "the peasant is stupid, but how should he become clever, unless he is accidentally so by nature? Yes, the peasant is lazy, but what would industry avail him, it would never lead him to prosperity. His industry would benefit the master rather than himself. Yes, the peasant still takes the penny he earns today to the tavern, but this wastefulness proceeds from his misery. Misery is not frugal, misery cannot even grasp a thought so sane and fruitful as that of frugality."

Countess Aniela raised her graceful head and her lovely lips assumed a mocking expression.

"Honored saviour of my life, you talk exactly like the emissary," she observed, "it seems like hearing him speak."

The doctor remained silent; the playful reproach struck home.

An hour later he was standing in his nursery in front of a sapling which, no thicker than one's finger, yet bore under its crown of leaves three beautiful apples, almost fully ripe, with yellow, glistening skins. Any other time he would have taken pleasure in the sight; today it only heightened his ill-humor. Joseph came out of the house, his implements on his shoulder, and wanted to show his benefactor some saplings just as ambitious to become sturdy trees as the one that had aroused the doctor's admiration.

The doctor remained unresponsive. Turning his eyes, glowing with grim severity under their bushy brows, upon the youth, he said abruptly:

"Tell me, have you never heard anything about a champion of freedom, a sort of fool, who is staying in the neighborhood, and, they say, is preaching revolution to the peasants?"

Joseph was evidently startled, and remained silent.

"Confess! Confess!" commanded Rosenzweig, and he bent his threatening countenance, flaming with anger, close to that of the youth.

"I don't know," stammered the latter, "whether you mean the one who is called the emissary."

"He is the very one I mean!"

"But he does not preach revolution, he preaches diligence and sobriety."

"Diligence in stealing, sobriety in killing — eh?" scoffed the doctor.

Contrary to his wont, Joseph was not to be disconcerted. He went still further — he actually presumed to contradict the doctor.

"You are mistaken. I know him."

Rosenzweig started back with an inarticulate cry, and Joseph continued:

"I had a long talk with him."

"Where? and when? and about what?"

"In the field last week; and the talk was about you."

" — About me?"

"He obtained his information about me from the *cha-mer's* lips?" reflected the doctor. — "Well, that is the way they are!"

"I have never heard him preach," resumed Joseph.

"But you should like to?"

"Oh yes! — I should like to. No preacher can equal him, they say. They say, too, that he will speak tonight for the last time in our neighborhood, in Abraham Dornenkron's tavern, a mile from here, on the road to Dolego."

A long silence followed, which was broken by the doctor, who ordered Joseph to proceed with his work; he himself repaired to the prefect, reported what he had just learned regarding the emissary, and asked whether it would not be advisable to send a detachment of hussars to the tavern and have the agitator arrested.

"All will be done that is necessary, my dear Rosenzweig," answered the official. "We have exact information of everything that is going on, and find no occasion for anxiety. What are you afraid of? You are one of us. I wish I could instill some of your caution into those who stand more in need of it than you and I."

Rosenzweig then paid a few professional visits and only returned home late in the evening. In front of the garden-gate he met Joseph, who was awaiting him.

"What are you standing there for? Go to bed," he called to him harshly.

He would gladly have found rest himself, but it fled from him on this night as it had on the preceding ones.

Suddenly the thought struck him that Joseph might possibly be stealing away from the house to hasten to the tavern in order to hear the agitator's farewell address. The distance, it is true, is great, and the evening far advanced, but the fellow has young limbs. ... For that matter — who knows! If he is afraid of being late, he may even take a horse from the stable. ... Well, at least *that* doubt should not trouble him long. Quickly seizing a candle from the table, he hurried down the steps and along the hall toward the room that Joseph occupied.

It was years since he had entered it; it was the only poor room in the house and irritated him every time he saw it. A narrow oblong chamber with a brick floor, lighted by a single window. Had Rosenzweig been Joseph's doctor instead of his "benefactor," he would have forbidden him to sleep on that straw-bed in the corner between the turning-lathe and the wall, which fairly dripped with dampness.

He said this to himself when he found the youth who he presumed was on his way to Dolego, stretched out in deep, blessed slumber upon his more than modest couch.

As Rosenzweig bent over him and turned the light upon his face, his eyelids quivered, his fresh, rosy mouth contracted defiantly, but only for an instant, then with lips lightly closed, he continued his peaceful breathing. Had he possessed a thousand tongues, they could not have pleaded more eloquently for his purity of heart than did the expression of unconscious, silent peace on his countenance.

Depositing the candle on the turning-lathe, the doctor looked round the room. The pieces of work he saw there, begun, half-finished, or nearly completed, all were the fruits of the industry of busy, skilful hands. And it must, after all, not have been such a poor brain that directed their execution, for nowhere was there any trace of wasted materials or childish trifling. And the young fellow's every thought was bent upon the prosperity and improvement of the doctor's home; that object absorbed all his efforts, commanded his best strength and insight. One example among a hundred struck the doctor particularly and — almost touched him.

The doctor had lately had the little wooden garden-gate replaced by an iron one and had been satisfied with the work of the local locksmith, but Joseph thought: "It is not pretty enough, I want to add some decoration." Rosenzweig laughed at him at the time, but now the work was under way, the ornament had with infinite pains been cut and filed out of heavy sheet-iron, and the doctor's monogram, quite artistically intertwined, stood out among graceful arabesques.

Rosenzweig smiled, crossed his arms, and, for the first time, sank into a kindly, sympathetic contemplation of this modest Jack of all trades. At the head of his bed he noticed a Saint Joseph, fastened to the wall by four nails, and below the picture in clumsy writing:

"From my Lubienka."

Yours, you poor fellow who own nothing on the broad earth? Have some solid soil under your own feet first before you dare call to a weaker mortal: Come to me! You have as yet acquired nothing, earned nothing in spite of your zealous industry and loyalty, nothing—no wages, no thanks, no rights. What you do for me, the use you are to me, serve only as payment for the involuntary debt you once incurred.

When will that debt be finally canceled, poor fellow? ... Has it in reality not been canceled long since? If you were clever enough to calculate and balance accounts, you would have said years ago: We are quits! From now on pay me, master! I, too, want to earn for myself. I am a hard man, they say, but no one dare call me unjust. If you had asked I should have given. I should have allowed you a place in the world, had you asserted yourself. But you did not; you kept on silent under your yoke and you will continue to go on the same way until you break down. You will be in as helpless a condition at the close of your life as you were at its beginning. ... Whose the fault! Why do you not reflect! Why do you not speak! Why do you waste the precious powers of your youth? ... But so it is, and I exploit them — and as I do, so do thousands, hundreds of thousands of others. ... One more glance at the peacefully sleeping lad, and Nathaniel closed his eyes and pressed his hands against his brow. A light, sharp and blinding as a sudden flash in the darkness, pierced his mind. He was filled with horror end dismay as the thought struck him: Here he lies still, calm and innocent, and hundreds of thousands like him are sleeping as he is. Yet they will awake — they are already being aroused. To what deeds? How will they act, these suddenly unshackled serfs!

A dizziness seized him; he felt as if his house were tottering.

"Not yet!" he cried, and he stamped the floor in passion.

Joseph awoke and sprang up: "What do you command, master!" His consciousness was no sooner restored than this question leaped to his lips.

"I want to know what is going on, what is being preached to you folks. I want to hear the emissary. Hitch up the horses; you will drive to the Dornenkron tavern. Hitch up!"

IV

The night was dark. A fine, close rain was falling steadily, and a liberal splashing was the result of the energetic tramping of the sturdy animals. "Poland's fifth element" enveloped and besprinkled the vehicle that Joseph was driving between a double row of giant poplars on the Kaiserstrasse.

The doctor, wrapped in his cloak, sat silent a long time. He was consumed with impatience.

"We shall be too late," he said finally. "Whip up the horses."

"They are running as fast as they can," answered Joseph. "We have gone a good way." He pointed to a great whitish spot on the leaden-gray horizon: "The Vistula and the Dujanec are hanging their flags out already."

A quarter of an hour later they reached their destination—a low, straggling building. All sorts of vehicles were standing in front of it, preventing Joseph from approaching.

Rosenzweig ordered him to stop, alighted and endeavored to make his way through the tangle of wagons and horses. It was no easy task for one who wanted to enter the house as unnoticed as possible.

Most of the drivers had left their vehicles, the others were, or pretended to be, asleep on the box, and paid no attention to the doctor's orders to allow him room to pass. He had just raised his stick to make his meaning clearer, when Abraham Dornenkron, with a burning torch in his hand, made his appearance in the doorway.

"Get them to make room, Abraham," said the doctor, "it is I, Doctor Rosenzweig."

"Great Heavens!" ejaculated the host in alarm; quickly collecting himself, however, he plunged obligingly into the swamp which formed the driveway to the inn. He made a breach into the stronghold composed of vehicles, calling at the same time with superfluous lungpower:

"It is Doctor Rosenzweig!—Is anybody sick? Where are you going, Doctor?"

As soon as there was a possibility of approaching him the doctor flew at him and caught him by the ear.

"Be still, you rogue. You need not announce me to your guests. I shall attend to that myself."

And as the little man continued in spite of this to proclaim aloud his astonishment at the doctor's advent, the latter jammed him against the doorpost until he could not breathe, and then passed by him into the hall.

"A gibbor!* Shema Israel, a gibbor, that powerful doctor," whispered Abraham to a misshapen creature, bow-legged like a goblin, who turned up suddenly in the darkness silently as a lizard.

He moved his ill-shapen head to and fro, his intensely black eyes sparkling with cleverness and fire.

"He has come here to play the spy, daddy dear. We'll steal a march on him, so that no misfortune can befall us," whispered the little man.

"Misery upon misery! How steal a march on him?"

"I'll take a horse, daddy dear, and ride to Tarnow swift as the wind to notify the police that the rebellious *Goim* are holding a meeting here, and that the Imperial Government should send the military against them, if the Imperial Government is so disposed."

Abraham contemplated his offspring with a glance of admiring love.

"Ride like the wind, my dearie, so that you may, God willing, soon reach your destination. Ride," he repeated, and added with naïve concern: "But take care that nothing happens to your straight limbs."

Rosenzweig had meanwhile entered, or rather forced his way, into the inn-parlor. A heavy, musty atmosphere pervaded the room, produced by the crowding together of more than a hundred people in wet furs, clothes, and boots. The fumes of liquor and the smoke of a night-lamp suspended from the ceiling contributed their share toward rendering breathing more difficult. Those present, however, experienced unconsciously the oppressive influences which made some faces glow and others turn pale as death. There were men of all ages and stations,

---

* A giant.

in poor garb, in the rich national costume, in the priest's robe, the student's coat, in the shabby black raiment of the petty scribe. Those who had come too late to find a seat stood on benches and, jammed between the crowd and the wall, they paid, at every new onrush, for the advantage of their elevated position, by the danger of getting crushed.

In the front row, towering above those about him, stood a gray-haired, broad-shouldered man in the rich costume of a grandee. As he turned his head, Nathaniel perceived the expressive Asiatic profile of one of the powerful princes of the country.

"You, too, Starosta, *princeps nobilitatis?*" thought Rosenzweig. But a still greater surprise awaited him.

The only space left free in the room was that which led into the adjoining apartment, the open door of which was guarded by a number of young people with a fiery zeal against the importunity of curiosity or fanaticism. And there Dembowski was walking up and down, engaged in conversation with a Polish gentleman in whom Rosenzweig, to his infinite astonishment, recognized the intimate friend of the prefect. Happy in his domestic life, and comfortably circumstanced financially, he was an inoffensive, upright man who prized peace above all things. He had never even succeeded in following a political debate of his neighboring land-owners to its close, for he regularly dropped asleep. And here, walking by the side of the agitator, was this most peaceful and calmest of citizens, burning, glowing in a spiritual conflict whose agony was depicted on his quivering countenance.

Dembowski, his figure slightly inclined, his hand lightly resting on the neophyte's arm, was speaking in a low, insistent tone, uttering thoughts to which his companion appeared unable to say anything in reply. A final word—then he turned from the man, he had thrilled and stepped in front of his followers, who greeted him with boundless enthusiasm.

The emissary was dressed like a peasant. He wore a long white caftan fastened at the throat by two large metal buttons, high boots, a shirt of coarse linen, and wide breeches of the same material. A leather belt, from which there hung a small ebony crucifix, encircled his waist. His thick, dark-yellow hair was cropped close; it came to a sharp point over his forehead and was finely arched about the dull whiteness of his somewhat hollow temples.

He waited calmly till the welcoming outburst should cease, his arms dropped at his side, his fingers lightly crossed, and he gazed carelessly, superficially into the throng, as near-sighted people are apt to do, who, in looking, renounce in advance the idea of seeing.

"Friends, brothers," he began, without raising his voice, and at once there was a hush of perfect silence— "I greet you for the last time before the struggle, perhaps the last time before death."

"Hail to you!" responded a dark-looking fellow with a martial air, "in struggle, in death, in victory!"

"In victory!" The cry ran through the throng as a sigh of longing, a cry of hope, an ejaculation of confidence.

"Victory?" repeated the orator, "you have already achieved it. A struggle such as yours is a victory, and each one of you a victor, whether he plant his foot upon his foes or lie trampled by their chargers on the battle-field. Brethren! whatever fate may be in store for us, the thought that inspires us cannot perish. It will live on, even on the lips of those who persecute and kill us on its account. They themselves will live to spread the sacred doctrine, in recounting the martyrdom that we have suffered."

Gradually the paralyzing fatigue left him; his supple form rose to its full height:

"Perhaps the memory of our death will be the only thing we can bequeath to those for whom we should so gladly have lived. We must see to it that that heritage shall be a glorious one. It will be no glorious one unless each one who has sworn allegiance to our league feels himself a priest whose ambition is renunciation, and his glory unstinted devotion to the cause of God."

Sounds of approval were to be heard here and there, but disappointment was written on many countenances.

"The cause of God, my brethren!" repeated the orator. "I would I had the power to rouse the fiery zeal in your hearts which it has roused in mine, and make you realize the abhorrence and shame with which I look back upon the worldly pleasures I once enjoyed. In the plenitude of their enjoyment the Master found me. I was roused from the dizzy whirl by His call. And the voice with which the All-merciful summoned me was the voice of compassion, and compassion gave birth to doubt, and doubt to knowledge."

As he spoke his countenance became transfigured, the light of loving, generous thoughts shone upon his brow.

"I lived the life of a spoiled child of fortune. Because chance had lavished too much upon me, I never knew satisfaction, gold melted in my immaculate white hands.

"There was one among my servitors — his name was Jelek — a peasant's son, who, alert and efficient, had risen to the position of steward of my estate. He alone dared upon one occasion to give me a warning and he incurred my disfavor in consequence.

"One summer morning, after a night of gayety, I was riding home with my followers from a fete at the house of my beloved. Her kisses were still burning on my lips, the tones of the music still rang in my ears, alluring visions floated before my eyes, I was filled with a rapturous joy of life. The remembrance of past pleasures was blended in my mind with the expectation of those to come, and in my arrogance I cried to my companions: 'As today so tomorrow and always!'

"We had reached the edge of the forest; before us lay the meadows fresh with dew, in the shimmering vapor of the young day, the waving fields of grain, and my castle with its sturdy towers, decked with streamers, beckoning us in the distance. Its windows were glistening; its walls, hoary with age, were illumined by the brilliance of the rising sun as a smile illumines the face of an old man. My venerable, hospitable dwelling presented a fine sight, and my companions galloped toward it with exultant shouts.

"I, however, reined in my impatient horse.

"I had seen a man hurrying along the edge of the wood, and recognized him as Jelek, my steward.

"'Whence and whither?' I questioned him. He named a distant farm to which the superintendent had sent him on an errand. — 'Was there no one in a lower position to attend to it? Since when do you go on errands?' — 'Since I incurred your displeasure your superintendent has dismissed me from my office and gives me all kinds of tasks in place of it.' — He was panting and wiping the perspiration from his brow, and I could see that the ground was burning under his feet. I saw also that a long procession was marching from the village toward the highroad, and that it was this he was striving to join. I started to walk my horse and Jelek followed me. Thus we reached the highway along which the people were tramping. There were a couple of hundred men, youths and old men, their scythes on their shoulders, sacks upon their backs. They strode on in silence, with heads bowed, most of them barefoot and ragged — my peasants! ... And as they, bowing to the earth, trailed past me, joyless as a herd driven to strange pastures, this fact was borne in upon me: These people are hired out for the harvest-time, far away perhaps, and will not behold the soil upon which their own poor crop is ripening until it is covered with snow.

"Jelek had pulled out a small kerchief in which he had tied a few coins, and pressed it into the hands of an old man who was dragging painfully along in the rear of the procession: — 'So that you may not be in want on the way, father. May God comfort you. It is on my account that you have to leave.'

"The old man hid the kerchief in his breast, and the Haiduk who directed the troop shoved him forward.

"Tears of sorrow and rage filled Jelek's eyes.

"'Why did you say,' I questioned him,' that your father had to leave on your account? '

"'Because it is the truth. The superintendent would not have dared to hire him out if I still enjoyed your favor as I used to.'

"A few days later I met Jelek as he was berating a field-hand, an aged man, for idleness, and beating him cruelly.

"'Don't you see that the man is exhausted and is unable to work any longer?' I said, and he answered:

"'That's the way my father will be treated away from home. Why should the one be better off than the other?'

"I knew not what to reply, but to the old man I said:

"'Don't the blows hurt you, that you stand there and do not even complain? '

"'Oh gracious sir,' he rejoined, 'what would complaining help me?'

"And to that, too, I could say nothing. ...

"In the evening my house was adorned for the reception of my beloved, and all who courted my favor were assembled to pay her homage. She appeared in all her regal beauty, and the sight of her and the sight of the magnificence that surrounded me and of the cringing

complaisance of my followers — abhorrence, my brethren. They aroused abhorrence within me. ... A demon
had, I thought, maliciously sharpened my eye to a terrible clearsightedness. All the brilliance, all the pomp
and splendor, and the love of woman and the loyalty
of friends — they had a price, and it was paid by misery.
Those had paid it who, hired out to compulsory service,
had gone off to strange places. ... The crowd around me,
the walls of the hall, became transparent. As through a
gleaming veil I beheld a tramping host, beheld clearly the
various ranks, every lineament of the faces upon which
that morning I had cast but a fleeting glance. Resignation
written upon them all! Not fine, manly resignation — no!
The disconsolate, hopeless resignation of dull despair.
What that victim of the unjust retribution inflicted by
my servitor had said, they likewise expressed by their
silence: what would complaint avail us?

"Brethren! In that hour I cursed my power and passed
sentence upon my happiness. ... My power had been exercised to the detriment of others, my happiness grew
not like a flower from the healthy womb of earth; it was
a rank growth, the fruit of its decay, and parasitically
nourished by the precious sap of human life."

The speaker threw back his head; his eyelids dropped,
he drew in his breath like a soul in torment.

"Then a stream of sorrows flooded my breast. ... The
sorrows of every one who had suffered on my account
poured into my heart! ... And every shortcoming, every
wrong committed by those in my service, I felt to be my
fault, and heard with shuddering how their cry rose
against me to heaven.

"The air in the hall hung heavy as lead, sin looked
forth from the eyes of my beloved, the music warbled
bewildering melodies, and — I felt I must away, away
from the dispelled delusion into the cool, clear night.
I wandered under its glistening stars as far as my feet

would bear me, and though my heart wrestled and bled, I felt as if I had been restored to life. In the bitter agony through which I was passing, I felt the hand of my Master, comprehended the warning which He had vouchsafed me. And while they were searching for me in the castle and the gardens, I was lying prone in the depths of the forest before my God, and prayed that strength might be given me for repentance and expiation, offered myself to Him as an instrument of His will, a promulgator of His teachings, and besought the primal source of light to illumine my path.

"And it was vouchsafed me. As the old, familiar, though unseen, world was disclosed to the eyes of the man born blind, when the Saviour touched them with His hand, so was disclosed to me the revelation in whose light I had been wandering from my youth on — a blind man. And the deeper I penetrated into the spirit of the divine word, the more clearly did it appear to me that the essence of its wisdom is love. For us mortals — brotherly love."

The swelling waves of enthusiasm with which the emissary had been greeted had gradually subsided. A murmur of disapproval, mingled only with a few scattering cheers, now ran through the assembly. From the group that crowded about the prince a rude voice cried:

"Let the preacher speak of brotherly love, speak you of the liberation of our fatherland."

"They are one and the same!" rejoined the orator. "No liberation without brotherly love. It is the inestimably precious treasure which will redeem us the moment we decide to unearth it. Only you must understand the law that governs it. For you, the powerful and the rich, its first words are: renunciation, privation, atonement!"

A smile played about the lips of the prince, but, with a voice growing ever stronger as he proceeded, the speaker continued:

"There is but one Master, the King of heaven and of earth, and but one people, born equals. He who arrogates a mastery over his brethren sows and reaps evil, the souls of the enslaver and of the enslaved become corrupted."

With rapid steps he approached the prince:

"Save your soul, humble yourself! Remember the sins of your fathers, remember the curses that lie heavy upon your head. What! You demand deliverance from foreign tyranny? What have you ever practiced upon your wretched people but tyranny? You, the nobility, were the State. Never in Poland did any class but yours have any say, and to what did you reduce the country! ... Your selfishness exploited, your dissension disrupted, your treachery delivered it to the enemy!"

"You lie! Keep quiet! We don't want to hear any more!" was shouted back at him.

A wild tumult arose.

"Room there! Room for the prince!" cried the attendants of the magnate, who had turned around silently and contemptuously, and for whom the attendants were attempting to open a way out by pushing and crowding.

Nathaniel, who was standing near by, proved himself helpful. The throng was wedged in, as it were, in the doorway, but his iron arm divided it so as to make a passage for those pushing forward, and there was a general sigh of relief when the prince with his train had succeeded in reaching the open.

From outside came the sound of their cries, curses, laughter. The gentlemen whistled for their drivers and their dogs, whips cracked, vehicles were started up.

The emissary's glance swept sorrowfully over the thinned ranks of his followers.

"I did not count upon the great of the earth; well for us had we no other antagonists," said he calmly, "The

68

oppressors are few, the oppressed many. Were the oppressed to rise and demand, in the name of the All-just, their share in the possession of the earth, the might of the mighty would be as chaff. But the colossus that would only need to stir to burst his bonds—he does not stir. He endures and serves, and will ever endure and serve. Through the life of indignity which he has led for centuries, the consciousness of his manhood, of his free will, has been stifled in him. But those who have robbed him of this consciousness have sinned not only against the wretched populace, upon whom they look with disdain, but—and they do not bear this in mind—against God, in that they have incapacitated thousands of his creatures from reflecting His image."

He paused and the younger people burst into vociferous cheers. The older men remained silent. Several ecclesiastics had retreated to the door. The disloyal friend of the prefect had disappeared along with the noblemen, after he had, with astonished dismay, beheld Rosenzweig's huge head looming up among the throng. The doctor, however, pressing against the man in front of him with the force of a pillar, gradually succeeded in making the latter give way, and was now standing on the spot previously occupied by the prince, directly in front of the emissary.

A flush of pleasure suffused the latter's countenance on perceiving Nathaniel.

"God will judge the guilty!" he resumed. "Our part is the deliverance of the poor, whose misery we are better able to gauge than they themselves. What I demand of you, masters, you know well; we have discussed it over and over again in long sessions. But you, students and men of science, who stand as close to the people as you do to your fathers, take care of them as if they were your children. Teach them to confide in and to love you; apply your knowledge, your skill, your experience, your strength and your time in their behalf. Forget yourselves in their service. None of you should henceforth cultivate his mind in cold seclusion. ... By what right do you plunge into the investigation of the most difficult problems of the universe, of existence, while around you there are still people, endowed with claims to knowledge equal to your own, who are incapable of formulating the simplest train of thought? ... You are seeking ends in your sciences but you will always find only boundaries. I will name an end to you which can be reached: the diminution of error, of delusion, of superstition, among our brethren. ... The pilgrimage of the human race over the earth is like the march of a vast army that breaks camp at night to hasten to the field of battle. Those to whom strength has been given to outstrip the others have put themselves at the head. They are already advancing in the rosy morning light, the shadows flee, a land of wonders is opening before them. Irresistibly they are speeding toward it on their radiant course, regardless of the rear guard which is groping about and going astray behind them, unable to find the path that leads to the happy ones by whose side they too were summoned to fight the battle of life. ... Therefore, ye leaders, halt! Open your ranks, let the rearguard come up. A broad path for the rearguard! For their salvation, my brethren! But also for yours, for Heaven will greet you from eyes hitherto dim, which, thanks to your thoughtful love, shall have been opened to admit a ray of the truth."

Some pedagogues close to Rosenzweig exchanged significant glances: "I am greatly disappointed," whispered a lawyer's clerk to the learned gentlemen; "it really amounts to nothing."

By and by the doctor was standing very comfortably; there was no question of crowding any longer. The audience left the room slowly and quietly. One vehicle after another drove off, the horses trotted away.

Those who remained finally tried to stop the exodus. The imprecations which followed the deserters began to turn into violence.

The orator raised his arm with a commanding gesture.

"Let every one go his way unmolested," he bade them. "Which of you can tell whether the little seed of truth which seemed now to rebound from the breasts of these men, has not, unconsciously to themselves, taken root there? Many a one, perhaps, of those who are leaving us now, may yet join our ranks some future day. As for me, my brethren, I feel it a blessing that in this hour of parting I am surrounded by fidelity, heard with understanding. The deepest significance of my precepts may I pour into your hearts as into precious vessels which will keep them pure and unsullied and impart them thus to other hearts.

"Brothers, we are always being told that without conflict among men the world could not exist; in a universal peace our energies would rust and our mind become enervated. That is false. Peace among men does not, indeed, mean the end of all conflict; it means, on the contrary, the beginning of a new, a glorious conflict. While hatred has been the author of all conflicts thus far, love will be the mother of those of the future. The combatants whom she summons will have by no means an easy task, for the enemies that confront them grant their conquerors no peace, no rest; conquered every day, they arise every day anew. *Suffering* and *passion* are their names. Fix your eyes upon them well, and you will be obliged to ponder and ask yourselves: Is it possible that we ever engaged in any other warfare but the one against the sufferings of others and against the passions in our own breasts? What—these terrible forces exist in the world, and we have concluded a hollow peace with them! We have accepted them as necessary and inevitable, we have drowsily allowed the vampire to feed upon our vitals and have not indulged our fighting propensity upon *them,* no, but upon our brothers, our fellow-sufferers! We have piled new burdens on the heavy-laden, we have struck the wounded.

"Oh the madness of it! Or the crime—or rather both! Crime is madness, folly is the source of every injustice."

Yes, a thousand times yes, reflected Rosenzweig, with tears in his eyes, shaken in every fibre of his being. He was penetrated by a boundless happiness, experienced the loftiest of all joys—the joy of rising from the narrowing limits of egotism as from a grave. What he had prized most hitherto appeared worthless to him now, wasted the labor that he had expended upon the acquisition of his wealth, despicable the narrow-hearted pleasure he had taken in what had lain dead, like so much dust, in his hands. His soul was filled with shame, but he surrendered himself to this feeling with ecstasy since it was the token of his transformation, of the beginning of his inner growth and purification. One thought alone clouded the serene beatitude of the moment; it concerned the apostle of compassion and love, and grew more painful and anxious, when the latter began to picture the future of which he dreamed as attainable.—"Do not deceive yourself!" the doctor would have liked to cry. "Your Land of Promise has no place on earth. Be content to have awakened our longing for it. That in itself is deliverance."

But the emissary continued. The sound of his voice filled the room as with a bodily substance, the fiery stream of his eloquence attained its boldest, most magnificent flights, and finally he concluded:

"The end and aim of our league is the welfare of the people, the welfare of every dweller on Polish soil; swear fidelity to our league!" Then all called out, the tone of a common inspiration ringing in the cry which burst from young and old, the experienced and the inexperienced, the prudent as well as the fanatical:

"We swear!"

They prostrated themselves before him and kissed his hands, his knees, his feet. "We swear obedience to you unto death!" one man's voice cried above all the rest. The emissary demurred:

"Not obedience to me—swear to the cause, to love the poor and oppressed as yourselves, and the Fatherland more than yourselves."

The protestations were renewed.

"And now go your way. Recruit among the people, raise recruits to do likewise. Send out no one who has not sworn upon the cross. I bring you the form of the oath and the catechism," said the agitator, and silence reigned while the tracts were being distributed.

Suddenly it was broken by a shriek of distress that startled all. Abraham Dornenkron rushed in, deathly pale, with disheveled hair:

"Let everybody save himself who can! My sonnie has been in Tarnow; he saw the hussars mount; they will be here soon, my sonnie rode ahead of them."

Abraham's warning aroused derision, defiance, consternation. Some stammered a low word of parting and hurried out. Those that carried arms gathered round Dembowski, prepared to defend him. He, however, motioned his faithful followers from him.

"Away! You, I, all of us. The time for battle has not yet struck. An arch-traitor every one who begins the battle too soon. Away! All away!"

The room was soon emptied. The last to leave was the emissary, Nathaniel stepping close before him. In profound silence the conspirators mounted their vehicles and vanished like shadows. The orator's horse was brought forward, he swung himself up and dug in his spurs. The animal reared, fell heavily on one of its forefeet and drew the other up with a quiver of pain.

Rosenzweig rushed to the spot. "Your horse is lame," he said, "you will make but little headway with it."

The inn-keeper came up, carrying a bottle containing a dripping tallow-candle, squatted down on the ground and confirmed with moans the doctor's opinion. A suspicion flashed across the latter's mind, he raised his clenched fist in the Jew's face:

"Wait, fellow, if you have done this!"

Abraham promptly burst forth into lamentations and protestations of innocence. The emissary had alighted from his horse, and stood motionless and listened.

The approach of the riders at full gallop could already be distinctly heard. They were accompanied by the keenly-whistling wind. A yellow-grayish shimmer began to appear on the horizon. The pale glow of opening dawn was spreading over the plain. Nathaniel grew hot and cold by turns. Cold perspiration covered his brow, his throat seemed caught in an iron clutch. *It was fear*, whose symptoms he had so often observed in others, and which he himself had never experienced.

"Conceal yourself in the house," he said to the emissary.

"What would that help me if the inn-keeper is false — and he is," answered the latter. "I will trust to my legs. As much cleverness as the hunted deer I too possess. Somewhere I shall find a cavern, a tree, a pitying bush, that will hide me."

He was about to start on his flight.

But the doctor seized him with overpowering strength and pushed him to his carriage.

"Down, Joseph," he commanded, "and see that you get home. But you, take his place. Quick!"

The reluctant emissary was lifted to the box before he was aware of it. The doctor threw the cloak which he had left in the carriage about Dembowski's shoulders, Joseph gave the reins into his hands and started homeward at once with rapid strides.

"You!" called Nathaniel, and Abraham bent almost to the ground under the doctor's lightning glance, "you will find out what I am if you continue to play the traitor!" Some imprecations followed which flowed readily from his lips. More difficult was it for him to add: "But if you hold your tongue—then you will get for your silence double what your tale-bearing would yield you."

He turned about rapidly toward the closely approaching riders.

"Ho, hallo!" he cried, putting his hands up to his mouth in the shape of a speaking-trumpet, "too late, too late."

A picket of hussars with a very youthful cadet at their head came galloping up. The cadet reined up his horse directly in front of Nathaniel:

"God's thunder! The doctor! What brings you here?"

"Curiosity, by Jove! my little count. But you—why just you! A hot ride in the early morning hours will give you, as sure as I know you, a sore throat."

"God's thunder! Don't jest! Am I really too late? Is the nest empty? Was the emissary really here? Did you see him?" questioned the young fellow with headlong haste.

"Saw, heard, and diagnosed him as a harmless enthusiast"

"Harmless? Then it was not he."

"It was."

"It was him," Abraham interposed glibly. "You can still see his horse, sir, which I lamed in shoeing it, so that he can't ride away."

"Which compelled him," Rosenzweig remarked, "to drive away in a friend's coach."

The youth inspected the horse, had the horseshoe removed, and ordered a soldier to take the horse along led by the bridle.

"I take it along as a pledge," he said. "And now—in what direction did he ride, doctor?"

"I would not betray that to you for any price."

"In what direction? The matter is grave. I am a made man if I capture him. We received more rigorous orders yesterday afternoon. — In what direction, doctor? ... God's thunder! Speak!"

Rosenzweig answered sullenly: "I know nothing. Perhaps you met him yourself on the road."

"I met nobody except some people whom I know well. ... For that matter" — he paused and pressed his hand to his brow. "They too are suspicious. ... Right about face!" he commanded his followers, and the hussars wheeled round. "Adieu, doctor. And you, Jew, mind this! A reward has been set on the emissary's head, a reward of a thousand gulden. It would have been yours, had I caught the fellow here."

Abraham started, wriggled like a worm, and uttered a loud shriek. The doctor's foot rested upon his and crushed it unmercifully.

"What is the matter?" cried the hussar.

"He is weeping for the thousand gulden which flew past his nose," returned Rosenzweig.

The cadet resumed his place at the head of his troop: "I shall ride back. The carriages we shall still overtake. ... God's thunder! We'll keep a sharp eye on them now. ... Gallop, march!" and the picket clattered off.

Abraham hopped on one foot and held the other, bent back, in his hand as if in a sling.

"Two thousand gulden!" he whimpered. "Doctor, you have mashed, you gibor, two of my toes. ... But I'll let that go, I won't ask for any damages if you pay me tomorrow my two thousand gulden, which you owe me as true as there is a God in heaven!"

Rosenzweig answered in a hollow voice: "Come now, you scoundrel. When I make a promise I keep it — even to a scoundrel."

He went up to the carriage and, pointing to the rear seat, said to his fellow passenger:

"Climb over there, and give me your seat. I shall bring you to a place of safety." The emissary with one bound stood by his side and grasped his hand warmly:

"I thank you. Do not concern yourself about me any further; I find friends everywhere."

In vain did the doctor seek to detain him; he disengaged himself, and was soon lost to the sight of his rescuer in the enshrouding half light of the dawn.

V

Rosenzweig drove home at a slow, easy pace—just as the horse pleased. He was in no hurry. Had the way been twice as long it would not have seemed too long to him. To one reflecting upon a miracle worked upon himself time passes swiftly.

Lied, duped, bribed a rascal—had he actually done these things, he, the upright Rosenzweig? Done them for the sake of a man whom he had regarded only a short time ago as an enemy of society, as his own enemy?

The most conflicting emotions were battling within his usually placid breast. But remorse, the worst of all, was not among them.

In the afternoon Abraham came to get his money. Yes, the rascal called it his, the precious money that was intended for the purchase of a new field. The doctor gave it to him with a sullen mien.

Then he betook himself to the prefecture.

He had meant to give his chief an exact account of the happenings at the tavern, but found him so busy and so unwontedly excited that he preferred to remain silent. The following days it was no better.

A constant agitation, an unusual activity pervaded the office. It was with difficulty that the prefect maintained his air of cheerful self-confidence. The assurance was forced with which he asserted that he held in his hands all the threads of the net in which Tyssowski in Cracow, Skarzynski in the Bochnian, Julian Goslar in the Sandec, Wolanski in the Jaslo, and Mazurkiewicz in the Sanoc districts, were entangled. The perfidy of his best friend, who had openly gone over to the revolutionary party, made a deep impression upon him. He and the doctor gradually changed parts. The anxious one became unconcerned, the unconcerned one anxious.

One morning Joseph handed his master a letter which had been brought to the house by a messenger. It contained two one-thousand gulden notes folded in a paper upon which were written these words:

"My debt to you can never be wiped out."

Nathaniel hid the sheet of paper in his breast and placed the notes in front of him on the table.

"Joseph," he called.

"What do you wish, master?"

"Look well at these pictures. Do you know what they represent?"

"Much money, I think."

"Money! Money! Well, yes—but something besides."

"What, master?"

"The reward of your long years of labor. ... No, not reward—the honestly earned proceeds."

Joseph cast an inquiring glance at his master.

"Look at *them,* at the pictures, not at me. They represent still a third thing."

"What, master?" repeated Joseph.

"What? Shall I call Lubienka? She would know at once that it can be nothing but—your marriage-portion."

Then Joseph exclaimed with a cry of ecstasy:

"My benefactor, my master, the kindest of men!" and wanted to prostrate himself before him.

"Stand up!" bade Nathaniel, laying both hands on his shoulders and gazing earnestly into his face, which was lifted to him as to a god.

"You have had a hard youth, my lad."

"I? — What are you saying, master? — Have you not always been like a father to me?"

"No, no, my boy, indeed not. But you have always been like a son to me," answered the doctor, and added what was incomprehensible to Joseph: "If there were many like you then the heavenly emissary would be no fool."

Thenceforth Joseph passed happy days, and they would have been still happier had not the great change which had taken place in his master caused him anxiety. It struck every one, and aroused the astonishment of all the doctor's friends. He, the eager economizer, was often seized by generous impulses. He who had always regarded a beggar and a thief as belonging to the same category, began to discover a great difference between them. He upon whom the rich and riches had hitherto exercised a strong fascination, visited the castles only when summoned, but entered the hovels of the poor unbidden. The restlessness which formerly had left him no peace had disappeared. With calm, persistent zeal he attended to his professional duties. When the revolution broke out and claimed its first bloody victims, he always managed to be where he was most needed. Never, not even in the darkest days, did the calm assurance leave him that there was nothing to be apprehended from the revolution.

The prefect was of a different opinion. While all courageous spirits were coming to the conclusion that the revolt must soon be ended, he still spoke of the province being lost unless an army were despatched in hot haste to fight the thousand-headed hydra of "devastating insurrection." He thought that Rosenzweig had lost his mind when he rejoined one day:

"The insurrection is no thousand-headed hydra, but a helpless child. It approaches with flowers in its hands, with a heart full of love, and words of deliverance on its lips. Thus does it come to us. But we are wolves, bears, tigers; we are ravenous beasts. We do not understand the language of this child. It preaches mercy, justice, and goodness, and we want to know nothing of all that, we want to have mercy upon no one but ourselves, we want to remain what we are, keep what we have, even take, if possible, something from others in order to enrich ourselves. And it will always be so, and he is a fool that doubts it! And we ravenous beasts will rend and devour the child and lie down to sleep satisfied after the heroic deed."

"Pure fantasies! Nothing but fantasies!" cried the official in consternation. "What has happened to you? What demon has confounded your sober senses?"

"Do you know," he resumed after a brief pause, "that it was reported to me that you had attended a meeting where the most dangerous of the communist leaders delivered one of his notorious speeches? Do you know that malicious scoffers assert that his eloquence made a fanatic of you?"

Nathaniel did not allow this accusation to disconcert him.

"I should be a fanatic," he rejoined, "if I believed in the possibility of realizing the Utopias for which this 'communist leader,' as you call him, lives and for which he will die. Well, not even under the influence of his presence, the music of his voice, the lightning-glance of his eyes, did the thought so much as flash across my mind: Who knows? Perhaps after all — ... Perhaps an example such as yours, may be able to teach us unselfishness and a general performance of the simplest duties. Oh, no, no! I know men too well for that. But what I did think was this: you will be knocked down, trampled upon, called a fool, and — forgotten. Ten years from now there will scarcely be one whom you loved who will mention your name. In spite of that, the powerful prince whom curiosity or the desire of making himself popular, impelled to attend your assembly, is a beggar compared with you. Only he who gives remains enduringly rich, and the greatness of a man is measured by the greatness of his thought and the sacrifices which he makes for it. Yours transcended the measure of what may be realized in our petty world. Its greatness turns it into error, and you into a visionary. Thus thought I; and I, the physician, the inveterate enemy and persecutor of everything morbid, eccentric, visionary, I sent up a prayer for him to my God: —

"Let him die encircled by all the creations of his folly, let him die unhealed, oh Lord!"

This prayer seemed to be answered before long in fullest measure.

The insurrection was frustrated by the resistance of the rural population; the body of men raised by the insurgents was beaten at Gdow by three hundred imperial troops and ten times that number of peasants who had joined them, under Benedek's energetic leadership.

Of this defeat the revolutionary Government at Cracow received distorted reports.

The champions of liberty, so ran the news, had been overpowered not by regular troops, but by fanaticized peasant hordes, which, having pushed on to Wieliczka, were now marching upon the city.

A cry of rage arose. It was silenced by the eloquence of a man who demanded forbearance for the misguided people, and asked to be sent to meet them as a missionary. That man was Edward Dembowski, and his wish was granted.

Relying upon the power of religion and of his eloquence he left Cracow, accompanied by priests in rich vestments, by monks bearing banners and crosses. A great mass of people followed, thirty sharpshooters bringing up the rear.

The procession crossed the bridge spanning the Vistula, and marched through the suburb Podgorze on the road leading to Wieliczka.

It lay still and deserted; as far as the eye could see, not a sign of any approaching peasant gangs. From Podgorze, however, came terrifying news, communicated to the rearguard by hasty messengers; it ran through the procession like lightning:

"Austrian troops are marching upon Podgorze."

A rapid command of the leader, and the procession started to retreat, in the hope of reaching the city before the imperial troops and of still being able to gain the bridge.

Arrived at the heights to the right of Podgorze, the emissary could already behold the storming of the town and the victorious advance of the soldiery.

The barracks were captured, the church occupied; the Polish riflemen, driven from their houses, were rushing in disordered flight toward the bridge.

Rage and grief filled the emissary's soul at this sight.

"Forward! Forward with the Lord, we'll fight our way through, we'll gain the bridge yet. Courage!" he cried to the hesitating priests. "You have nothing to fear. Those who are driven to attack put no heart into it. These men are Galicians, they will not shoot at their countrymen, they will not shoot at consecrated priests!"

He bade his followers strike up a hymn, and in stately order the procession descended the height. The emissary, clad in peasant costume, led the way, his light caftan glistening in the gathering twilight, a small black cross in his hand.

The procession marched unmolested through the still unoccupied part of the town to the church. But a company of soldiers had already pushed on to that point, barring their way to the bridge.

The emissary halted.

"Behold your brethren!" he addressed the soldiers and pointed to the bands that followed him. "You, too, are Poles. Don't fight, brothers — make way!"

He was answered by silence. He began once more to adjure the soldiers when the command rang out:

"Charge bayonets!"

With an expression of desperation Dembowski looked around him.

The priests and monks had fallen back. But his faithful adherents and the riflemen crowded about him.

"There is no way out of it. ... Shoot — and forward!" he cried suddenly, and fell upon the soldiers.

Two discharges answered the unexpected attack.

After the first, Dembowski was still seen standing upright, swinging the cross high above his head.

After the second he fell, shot in the head.

Rosenzweig heard of the emissary's death through the prefect, who wound up his report with the words: "A madman was bound to end like that."

Nathaniel's prophecy was fulfilled; the most idealistic representative of the revolution was unanimously censured and derided by all parties and his memory was soon forgotten among the people, too.

His body was not found among those who had fallen at Podgorze, and for a time it was maintained that he was not dead, that he lived in concealment as a peasant and would appear on the scene of new battles for freedom.

When the storms of 1848, however, broke out and subsided without having lured him from his supposed concealment, the hope of his return was extinguished even among those who had cherished it longest.

It was a mild September evening, at the close of the fifties, in a village a short distance from the Silesian border. In front of the tavern a covered britschka was standing, to which a pair of lusty bays were harnessed. Comfortably, leisurely, as befits hearty eaters, they were enjoying the contents of the feeding-trough set before them. The driver, an elderly man, as well-fed as his horses, had seated himself on a bench in front of the house, was sending out thick clouds of smoke from a short pipe, and took pleasure in answering the questions of the pretty barmaid with a roguish hesitancy, aimed at heightening the curiosity she already felt at the arrival of guests who were total strangers.

"You are traveling a long way, I suppose," she remarked.

"Further than you can imagine," he replied.

"Perhaps way into Hungary?"

"Pooh! That would be only a cat's leap! "

The girl put her arm to her hip and laughed: "I should like to see a cat that could jump like that! "

"In our place at home there are plenty such. You just come there and you'll see them."

"Oh what stuff! ... But where is your home?"

"Where?"

He pointed with his hand in three different directions: "There — and there, and there."

"Go along, you are joking."

"Ask my master, if you don't believe me."

"Yes, exactly," she rallied, "ask — such a gentleman!"

"Are you afraid?" — he winked at her slyly. "Have you already found out that he is a magician?"

Rapidly and furtively she made the sign of the cross: "Is that so? I shouldn't have thought it to look at him."

"Yes, a very great magician. Makes the sick well and brings the dead to life."

"The dead?" ... The girl shuddered.

"The half-dead, then. We are just on our way to one like that."

"Then you'll get there too late, if you have a long way to go yet."

"We never come too late. The master only says: Wait! — and death waits."

"Is that so? Has your master a wife?"

"He has no wife, but he has more than a hundred children."

"Listen to that!" and again she burst into a ringing laugh.

The subject of this colloquy was an old man of sturdy appearance. He wore a traveling-cap and a long coat, loosely fastened at the breast. The lower part of his strong, swarthy face was covered by a beard, which, white and thick as his hair, was divided into two strands and descended almost to his waist. The old man, his hands behind his back, was standing on the further side of the pond, which, situated a stone's throw from the inn, formed a long-drawn oval, at whose narrow extremity gnarled and crooked willows bent their branches to the murky mirror, while the other end grew gradually shallow toward the mounting village street.

The pond was all things in one — bathing-place for the young, washing establishment for the housewife, a lake for aquatic fowl, a watering-place for horses. In the evenings on week-days the place presented a lively sight. Big boys and small, barefooted, their trousers pulled up over their knees, rode their horses into the water, admired and envied by the children standing or sitting on the shore — mostly rather negligent guardians of their younger brothers or sisters. Men and women were returning home from the field, and, announced in advance by the tones of a resounding song, a troop of girls, carrying rakes and sickles, came marching to the village.

Among the children disporting themselves around the pond there was one that aroused the stranger's special attention—a little fellow of about six years, with a most winning but pallid face. His smooth, blond hair, long in the back and cut straight across his brow, escaped abundantly from beneath his little cap. He had deep-set blue eyes, a slim, slightly arched nose, and a sensitive, expressive mouth. Judging by the quality of his caftan and his boots, he belonged to well-to-do parents.

In the open doorway of one of the houses near by appeared a young and pretty woman with a child in her arms, and called to the boy:

"Jasin, father is coming."

Thereupon the little fellow turned a somersault and ran from his companions to meet his parent. The latter stood still, leaned forward and laughed as his little son ran full tilt against him. Straightening the boy's cap and taking him by the hand, he continued on his way.

It was delightful to see them coming along, the peasant and his child, the little fellow the miniature counterpart, in bearing, gait, and dress, of his father.

They came nearer, and the stranger noticed on the peasant's face the disfiguring traces of a serious wound. The right cheek was sunken and seamed with scars, the right eye closed.

Another veteran of the last uprising, reflected the old man, and fixed his gaze more and more attentively upon the approaching figure. A conjecture, strange and wonderful, flashed across his mind. Suddenly advancing a few steps, he stood still directly in front of the peasant, stared at him and cried:

"Is it possible?"

The peasant stepped back in astonishment but only to rush toward him the next moment.

"You! Good heavens! you—Doctor Rosenzweig!" exclaimed he, with a voice whose music had lived unforgotten in the old man's mind. Sooner than the doctor he regained his composure: "It was not in vain, then, that I have been expecting you, not in vain that I hoped you would take your way through our village on one of your Samaritan journeys, in order—" he added on account of the people around them—"to visit your servant Hawryl."

"Hawryl—" stammered Rosenzweig. "Hawryl, then ... How goes it with you, Hawryl? "

"You must see for yourself. Do me the honor of entering my home, rest awhile under my roof."

Silent, still quite stunned, the doctor accepted the invitation, and followed his host to the house, where upon the threshold the young woman had remained standing, and was striving to retain in her arms the lusty child, which was stretching its little hands to its father with shouts of joy.

"My dear wife, doctor," said Hawryl, and turning to her: "Bid him welcome, Magdusia, a worthier guest Heaven cannot send us."

Her countenance reflected, cordially and sincerely, the joy pictured on her husband's face. "A warm welcome to you, sir," she said, turning her smiling, true-hearted glance upon him.

Nathaniel felt as if in a dream. It was only when he found himself alone in the room with Hawryl that he began to recover from his amazement:

"You are alive!—Man, you are alive! Is it true that you are alive? But if it is true, then don't stand there so indifferent—"

"Indifferent!" exclaimed Hawryl.

"Well, give me your hand, then!"

For the second time he held it in his own—one different from before, a rough hand, whose owner did not merely *play* the peasant

They seated themselves at the table, which occupied the centre of the cheerful room, and it was long ere

Hawryl, interrupted again and again by the doctor's exclamations of astonishment, could conclude the singular, and yet simple, story of his deliverance.

He attributed it in the first place to the garb he wore when he was wounded at the church in Podgorze and left for dead. On discovering that he still had life in him, he, along with other country-people, was removed to the hospital at Cracow. There he regained consciousness and soon became convinced that the physician who treated him by no means took him for a peasant. Later, some words that the physician let fall, apparently without any object, betrayed to him that he was recognized.

On the day when he was declared cured, the director, a Pole, — the hospital management had not yet been changed — visited the convalescent room.

The agitator beheld this man for the first and last time in his life.

"Your name is Hawryl Koska," he said to him, "you come from the Kingdom and are a dependent of Count Bronski, who has transferred you to his Galician estate, to a peasant holding. That is what I read in your passport. Is that right?"

And without waiting for a reply he handed him a pass made out in the name, and bearing the personal description, of Hawryl Koska, and, turning to his neighbor, left the newly christened man standing there.

"In the most confused state of mind possible for a man to be in, I had positively expected to be summoned before a court upon my recovery and to be shot as one of the inciters to rebellion, and had prepared myself for death like a true Christian. And now I was to live. My first sensation was one of disappointment, my first thought an arrogant one: God is preserving you for a purpose. He does not want your death, He wants your service. The work which you were chosen to begin, you are also to complete.

"Filled with this proud belief, I mingled with the people and became their comrade; apparently an equal among equals, I was in my own vain sight a prophet in disguise. Oh my friend! a single year of that life, and the pretended prophet had become a humble man. The end that seemed within reach withdrew to immeasurable distances. The temple which I wished to crown with a splendid dome had not even had its corner-stone laid, nay, the ground had not yet been dug for its foundation. What was needed was not the work of the artist but that of the modest day-laborer.

"I realized that.

"And now — should I not have been a miserable blusterer had I disdained to take part in that work, that most important work? ... So I took hold of shovel and spade, not merely in a figurative sense. The crucifix, in the name of which I once went forth to battle, hangs there above my children's bed. Oh look at the outstretched arms of love, the wounded breast, the bowed, most noble head. ... Who dares presume to summon to strife and battle in the name of that intercessor?"

He heaved a sigh, but his countenance retained its expression of profoundest, serenest peace, and with a cheerful smile he continued:

"And it is thus that you find the dangerous agitator. Oh when I think of how I started out, of all that I hoped and believed myself capable of doing — and now! I retire to rest contented, and call that day happy when I have succeeded in keeping Jan from beating his wife, Martin from going to the tavern, and in persuading Basil to throw his old plow into the corner and drive to the field in the new one."

"But your secret," asked Nathaniel, interrupting the course of the narrative, "was there never any danger of its being betrayed?"

"The former owner of the land took it with him

into the grave. To his successor I am a peasant like any other."

—"A peasant! A peasant! ... And you mean to continue thus to the end?"

—"To the end; and I do not feel as if I were doing something great, or giving my neighbors more than I receive from them. I am by no means always their instructor; they are likewise mine. Their pleasures I cannot share, but in trouble and sorrow we have often been true companions. I have seen peasants standing before their fields covered with hail, I have seen mothers standing at the bier of their children, and have been awed. Barely has one of them appeared contemptible to me, but a hundred, innumerable times, deserving of pity."

His eyes shone with the old passionate fire, his swarthy cheeks turned pale with the depth of his emotion.

"There is a treasure-house of patience, perseverance, heroic submission to a higher will, in this people, which all the ill-usage they have experienced has been unable to exhaust. But, unconscious of their wealth, they scatter it around and add nothing to it. Insight is lacking and with it the exercise of active moral forces. Enough! Enough! you know all this as well as I, and likewise that there is plenty of work, not insignificant, to be done in my insignificant post. My capacity just suffices to fill it. Hawryl Koska will not have lived in vain. The *emissary* died without leaving a disciple."

"Yes, one!" cried Nathaniel. "One whom you drew from the ranks of your most zealous opponents. A man whose aims were of the earth, earthy, whose heart hung upon perishable possessions, and whom you taught the value of imperishable ones. Emissary! you see before yourself your white-haired disciple."

Both sprang to their feet at the same instant, and throwing themselves into each other's arms, held each other in a close embrace.

CONTENTS

Books published by Mondial

French Classics:

1. Rougon-Macquart Series:

Emile Zola: The Fortune of the Rougons
ISBN 1595690107 / 9781595690104

Emile Zola: The Fat and the Thin
(The Belly of Paris)
ISBN 1595690522 / 9781595690524

Emile Zola: Abbe Mouret's Transgression
(The Sin of the Abbé Mouret)
ISBN 1595690506 / 9781595690500

Emile Zola: The Dream
ISBN 1595690492 / 9781595690494

Emile Zola: A Love Episode (A Page of Love)
ISBN 1595690271 / 9781595690272

Emile Zola: The Conquest of Plassans
ISBN 1595690484 / 9781595690487

Emile Zola: The Joy of Life (Zest for Life)
ISBN 1595690476 / ISBN 9781595690470

Emile Zola: Doctor Pascal
ISBN 1595690514 / 9781595690517

Emile Zola: His Excellency
(His Excellency, Eugène Rougon)
ISBN 1595690557 / 9781595690555

Emile Zola: Money
ISBN 9781595690630

Emile Zola: The Soil (The Earth)
ISBN 9781595690883

2. Other French Literature:

Emile Zola: The Mysteries of Marseille
ISBN 9781595690913

Emile Zola: The Flood. ISBN 9781595690944

Emile Zola: Death. ISBN 9781595690937

Emile Zola: Fruitfulness (The Four Gospels)
ISBN 1595690182 / 9781595690180

Emile Zola: The Fête in Coqueville
(The Coqueville Spree) ISBN 9781595690869

Victor Hugo: Ninety-Three. ISBN 9781595690920

Victor Hugo: Bug-Jargal. ISBN 9781595690951

Victor Hugo: The Man Who Laughs
(By Order of the King)
ISBN 1595690131 / 9781595690135

Victor Hugo: History of a Crime
ISBN 1595690204 / 9781595690203

Voltaire: The Princess of Babylon
ISBN 9781595690999

Honoré de Balzac: Ursula (Ursule Mirouet)
ISBN 1595690530 / 9781595690531

Honoré de Balzac: Maitre Cornelius
ISBN 1595690174 / 9781595690173

Anatole France: Penguin Island
ISBN 1595690298 / 9781595690296

Anatole France: The Crime of Sylvestre Bonnard
ISBN 9781595690593

Gustave Flaubert: Salammbo (Salambo)
ISBN 1595690352 / 9781595690357

Romain Rolland: Pierre and Luce
ISBN 9781595690609

Jules Verne: An Antarctic Mystery
(The Sphinx of the Ice Fields)
ISBN 1595690549 / 9781595690548

André Gide: Strait is the Gate
(La Porte étroite) ISBN 9781595690623

André Gide: Prometheus Illbound
ISBN 9781595690807

André Gide: Recollections of Oscar Wilde.
ISBN 9781595690814

Alphonse Daudet: Little What's-His-Name
(aka Little Good-for-Nothing)
(Le Petit Chose. French Classics)
ISBN 9781595691057

German Classics:

Heinrich Heine: Germany. A Winter Tale
(Deutschland. Ein Wintermärchen.)
Bilingual Edition. ISBN 9781595690715

Heinrich Heine: The Rabbi of Bacharach
(German Classics) ISBN 9781595691002

Heinrich Heine: Florentine Nights.
(German Classics) ISBN 9781595691019

Heinrich Heine: From the Memoirs of Herr von
Schnabelewopski (German Classics)
ISBN 9781595691026

Johann Wolfgang von Goethe:
The Sorrows of Young Werther
ISBN 159569045X / 9781595690456

Theodor Storm: The Rider of the White Horse
(The Dykemaster) ISBN 9781595690746

Heinrich von Kleist: Michael Kohlhaas
(A Tale from an Old Chronicle)
ISBN 9781595690760

Gottfried Keller: A Village Romeo and Juliet
(Swiss-German Classics) ISBN 9781595690791

Gottfried Keller: Ursula
(Swiss-German Classics) ISBN 9781595690838

Gottfried Keller: The Governor of Greifensee
(Swiss-German Classics) ISBN 9781595690845

Wilhelm Raabe: The Hunger Pastor
(German Classics) ISBN 9781595690753

**Theodor Storm, Adelbert von Chamisso,
Adalbert Stifter:** Famous German Novellas of the
19th Century (Immensee. Peter Schlemihl. Brigitta.)
ISBN 159569014X / 9781595690142

Other books:

Agatha Christie: Two Novels (The Mysterious
Affair at Styles. The Secret Adversary.)
ISBN 1595690417 / 9781595690418

Jack London: War of the Classes. Revolution.
The Shrinkage of the Planet.
ISBN 1595690409 / 9781595690401

Jack London: Before Adam. Children of the Frost.
ISBN 1595690395 / 9781595690395

Jack London: The Iron Heel
ISBN 1595690379 / 9781595690371

Jack London: Burning Daylight.
ISBN 9781595691064

Oscar Wilde: The Critic as Artist. Upon the
Importance of Doing Nothing and Discussing
Everything. ISBN 9781595690821

Oscar Wilde, Anonymous: Teleny
or The Reverse of the Medal (Gay erotic classic)
ISBN 1595690360 / 9781595690364

Martin Andersen Nexo: Pelle the Conqueror
(Complete Edition: Boyhood. Apprenticeship.
The Great Struggle. Daybreak.)
ISBN 159569028X / 9781595690289

Martin Andersen Nexo: Ditte Everywoman
(Complete Edition: Girl Alive. Daughter of Man.
Towards the Stars.)
ISBN 9781595690333

Susan Coolidge: Clover
ISBN 1595690263 / 9781595690265

Jerome K. Jerome:
Idle Thoughts of an Idle Fellow
ISBN 1595690247 / 9781595690241

Malama Katulwende: Bitterness
(An African Novel from Zambia)
ISBN 159569031X / 9781595690319

Sigmund Freud: Dream Psychology
(Psychoanalysis for Beginners)
ISBN 1595690166 / 9781595690166

Gertrude Stein: Three Lives
(With an Introduction by Carl Van Vechten)
ISBN 1595690425 / 9781595690425

Gabriele D'Annunzio:
The Child of Pleasure. ISBN 9781595690581

Carl Van Vechten: Firecrackers.
A Realistic Novel. ISBN 9781595690685

Bruce Kellner: Winter Ridge. A Love Story.
ISBN 9781595690692

Donald Windham: Two People (Gay Classics)
ISBN 9781595691033

Frederick (Friedrich) Engels: Socialism: Utopian
and Scientific (Appendix: The Mark; Preface by
Karl Marx) ISBN 1595690468 / 9781595690463

Karl Marx: The Eighteenth Brumaire of Louis
Bonaparte. ISBN 1595690239 / 9781595690234